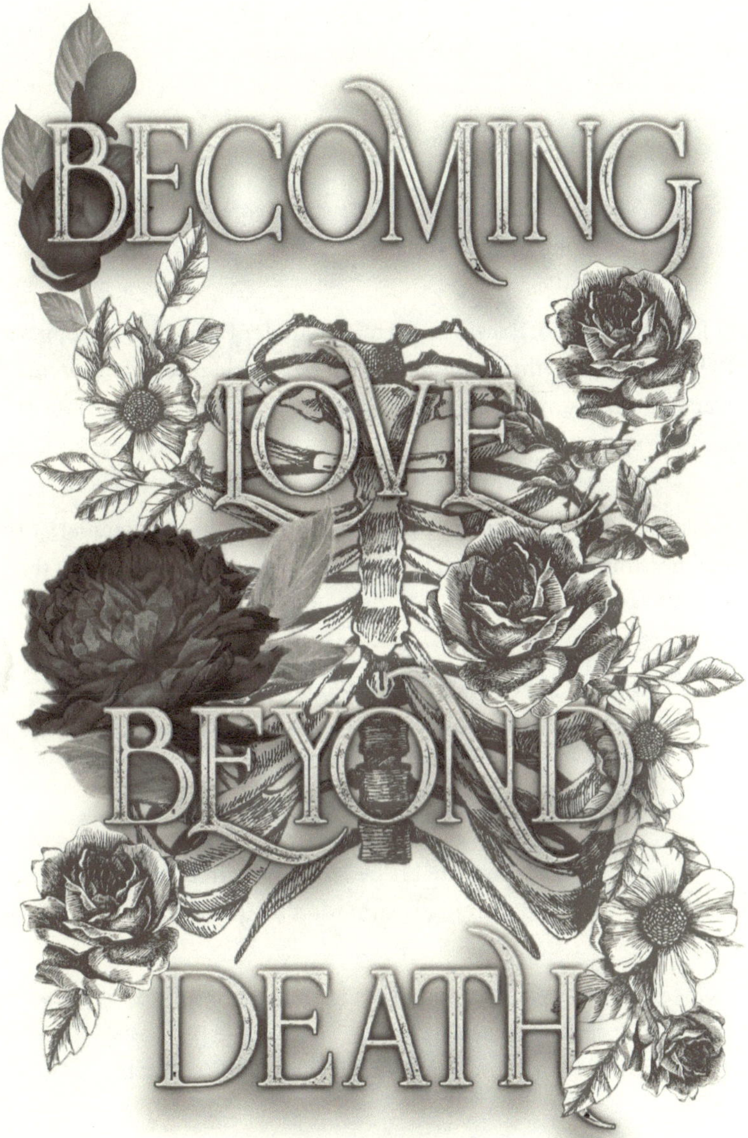

Becoming Love Beyond Death

AVA WIXX

Becoming Love Beyond Death

Becoming Love Beyond Death © 2024 by Ava Wixx

All Rights Reserved. Except as permitted under the U.S. Copyright act of 1976, no part of this publication may be reproduced, distributed, or transmitted in any form or by any means, or stored in a database or retrieval system, without the prior written permission of the author.

The characters and events in this book are fictitious. Any similarity to real persons, living or dead, is coincidental and not intended by the author.

First Edition: September 2024
Published in the United States of America by
Wicked Wixx Press.
The Wicked Wixx Press Logo is a trademark of
Wicked Wixx Press.
Originally published under the title
Becoming Death: March 2014

Cover Art, Ava Wixx Logo, Wicked Wixx Logo, & Interior Book Graphics by Lindsay Tiry of LT Arts
Edited by Melissa Ringsted of There For You Editing

Print ISBN: 978-1-955950-33-6
Kindle ISBN: 978-1-955950-34-3
EPUB ISBN: 978-1-955950-35-0

For more information visit: avawixx.com

Content Warning

Dear Readers,

If you've made it to this book in the trilogy then you already know what you're in for. For the most part. *wink*

But I'll reiterate anyways.

The characters in this three-book series are extremely flawed, which translates to a ton of questionable behavior. In other words, if you're not a fan of morally grey MCs who fuck up a lot, then you might not want to read this series.

And on that note, if swear words bother you, then this series might not be for you. (Personally, I don't think there are a lot of F-bombs or anything like that, but I cuss so much that I don't notice anymore. Although I do keep the language cleaner when I'm writing … it's easier to spot on page. *shrugs*)

Basically, this is not a light and fluffy story, but rather

a dark romance. Although in comparison to what's out there nowadays it's more dark-ish than anything.

Like I mentioned in the *Feeling Love Beyond Death and Embracing Love Beyond Death* warnings, this series gets darker as it goes along, and *Becoming Love Beyond Death* has even more of the death addiction intermingled with sex going on. I feel it's a natural progression within the storyline, but if the first two books were more than you could handle, I'd recommend not continuing the series.

Now that we have all of that out of the way, if you've decided to proceed … Happy reading!

~Ava

For all of you who were forged in darkness and pain, and yet still refused to give up.

DEATH IS THE ULTIMATE ADDICTION…

Prologue

This is a story of becoming.

Becoming what I was born to be.

Unfortunately, some destinies are much darker than others …

Chapter 1

The moment we're born we begin our journey towards death. An intelligent person knows this, accepts it, and makes the best of the time they have, knowing it's always finite. But an ignorant person ignores death, turns and presents their cheek, pretending that it doesn't exist.

Ignorance is bliss. It's an old saying most of us have heard enough times that it has ceased to have meaning. Not to me … at least not anymore. *I'm surrounded by death, and I wish I could pretend I wasn't.*

"Sam, snap the fuck out of it." Nixon's panicked voice pounded against my eardrums. "*Sam*!"

My lips flexed into a tight smile, but not directed at Nixon. I knew I was in the room with him physically, but the rest of me was elsewhere. "My good Sammy girl," Austin's seductive baritone purred, seeming to caress my very soul. "This is for you."

Intertwined with Austin's senses, it was as if we were one, both of us lost to the tumultuous death looming before us.

I luxuriated in the sensation of my fingers wrapping around the skinny neck, the Adam's apple bobbing with futility under my hands as my grip tightened. The cool spring evening brought with it the flavor of hope, energizing me with possibilities. A surge of euphoria dangled just out of reach, drifting closer with each moment as my victim gasped for air.

My victim—or in truth, Austin's victim—was a young man, not more than twenty-two, his thoughts entirely focused on the biggest regret of his about-to-be-too-short life. Loss—the loss of the one he loved, centering on the anguish of knowing what could have been if he were to live, and yet never would be now that death was near.

No ... no ... no ... Brandy. It can't end like this. She'll be waiting for me. I was going to propose tonight. I was going to make her my wife. Everyone said we wouldn't make it ... that we met too young, are still too young. But we would—we would have made it. I know we would have. We would have been so happy. Why? Why now? Why is this happening to me now? Tonight? Although I suppose it's better than after ... Will she move on? Or will she be too devastated? I wish I could tell her to move on. I want her to be happy, I just want to make her happy. It's the only thing I've ever really been sure about in my life. Her ... Brandy ...

"Fuck," Austin muttered. "Fuck, fuck, fuck. I can't fucking do it."

The last thing I sensed before our connection snapped

was that Austin had let his victim go, leaving him sputtering for air on the ground. But alive. He was still alive.

Equal parts disappointment and hope intermingled and swirled within my chest. I could still save Austin. It wasn't too late for him … even if it was for me. Because even now, he'd somehow managed to stop himself before taking the last step, plummeting himself over the edge. He'd yanked himself out of the death emotions at the last possible moment. Would I have been able to do the same? I shook my head harshly, wanting to dislodge the truth that lurked in the dark recesses of my mind.

Sitting up, I allowed my physical surroundings to settle into focus around me. I was in the tiny room Nixon had stashed me in, although a prison was a more accurate description since the space only fit a medium-sized bed and a chair. He was keeping me prisoner and attempting to control my life under the guise of protecting me … again. The entire concept made me want to laugh.

Glaring up at my jailor, I snarled, "Hands off."

Nixon let go of my shoulders reluctantly. "What the—"

I rolled my neck and sucked in a few centering breaths. "How long do you plan on keeping me here? Bigger picture, this is never going to work. You do realize that, right?"

His gaze darted away from me. "I'm going to fucking save you from him whether you like it or not. I'm—"

"Going to end up dead!" I jumped to my feet. "You

know he wants me with him now. He's going to come for me, and by you doing it this way— Fuck!"

Tugging at my hair, I eyed the walls around me as they seemingly bowed and shrunk. I'd never been claustrophobic before, but given enough time in my new cell, I would be. "Don't you get it? Right now, there's still hope. But I need to get to him—to save him. If you keep me here, he's just going to get worse, and he's going to drag me down with him. He hasn't crossed that final line yet, but he's a hairsbreadth away! He could cross it at any moment, and I can't let that happen!"

A sob erupted from my chest, twisting my insides. "Please. I can't fucking let that happen. Please, just please." Panic surged, constricting around my ribcage like a steel band. My entire body shook as I forced air into my lungs to continue speaking. "If you love me even half as much as you claim, you won't keep me here."

Nixon ground his teeth together, his jaw muscles popping. "No. You don't know what's best for you anymore." He abruptly shifted, giving me his back as he chuckled darkly. "And I'm beginning to think you never did."

He ambled a few steps away, pausing with his shoulders slumped. Then he made a sound as if he would say something else, but instead, he cleared his throat and reached for the doorknob to my prison—aka the only way to my freedom. Lurching from the bed, I jumped on his back, wrapping one arm around his neck as I pummeled my fists against his taut muscles.

I have to get to Austin. I have to save him.

Staggering to the side, Nixon still managed to swing around with relative ease, smashing me into the wall to trap me between it and him. His arm jerked out abruptly, slamming into me. A sharp sting registered in my thigh as an acid-like substance burned through my veins. I glanced down to see a needle protruding from my jean-clad leg just as a wave of dizziness assaulted me. A moment later, the edges of my vision began to dim.

"Seriously, where the fuck do you keep those?" I slurred. "You always—you can't possibly …"

All went dark.

Chapter 2

"Sam. Sammy, my good Sammy girl, I need you." Austin's raspy voice swirled around me, curling into my ears to touch, caress, and stir up the deep-seated yearning to be within his embrace. There were no accompanying images, just his nearly overwhelming desire for me to be with him.

Lying motionless on the bed in my new prison, I squeezed my eyes tightly shut, salty tears burning a trail down my face. The tone and tenor of Austin's voice held more than his simple plea did. He was on the precipice, staring off into the oblivion of death. He wanted to take that leap, unsure as to why he hadn't yet. Although it wouldn't be long before he would … he'd been so close earlier. The young victim only dodged death by the closest of margins thanks to the leanings of his emotions. Soon, Austin would kill an innocent with his own hands. He wanted it—the pleasure, the satisfaction, the relief. And yet …

"Austin," I choked out. "Hold on. Please, just hold on."

"I need you, Sam. I fucking need you so much." He was raw and desperate, reaching out for what meager comfort I could provide despite our physical separation.

Abruptly, his mood shifted, spiriting my hope away with it. "I want to enjoy my first kill with you. Think about how amazing it would be for us."

And I did. My mind turned to the dark yet euphoric memory of how it had been between us after the blast scene we'd visited—the first time we'd experienced death of that magnitude together.

I was alive ... so, so alive. Those deaths brought with them a euphoria that wasn't like anything I'd ever experienced before, and to add kindling to the fire, the love of my life was currently buried deep inside of me, sharing everything—connecting us in a way we'd never felt before. Heaven.

"Sam, Sam, Sam ... my Sammy girl," Austin's voice whispered in my mind. "Never stop. Need you."

His thoughts were fragmented, desperate. Regardless, I knew what he meant, and I felt the same way. "Never. I'll never stop loving you, touching you. Because you're mine. And I'm yours."

Death—all those deaths, and us linked as we felt them only served to heighten the frantic need to lose ourselves in each other. He thought I was dead only a short time ago, and I thought he was a figment of my imagination. But now, in this moment, none of that mattered. Having walked away from those deaths made us feel our lives more acutely, making us want to grab onto each other and never let go. Nothing else mattered but us, together in this moment. He was my world, and I was his. I needed to feel him ... feel all of him, mind, body, and soul.

I screamed my release in perfect unison with Austin's, but there was no reprieve from my excessive need for him. The flames of my desire crackled and burned, reaching higher. I needed more ... more ... more.

My hands roamed his sweat-glistening body, and my lips continued to sip at the sweet nectar that was his mouth. "Austin," I moaned. "Please."

"Yeah. Yeah, I'm with you, Sam. I'm with you," he murmured against my lips. He continued to pivot his hips until he stiffened inside of me with fresh excitement.

"Yes ... yes ... yes ..." I repeated on an unending loop, losing myself in Austin completely, because he would always be exactly what I needed.

My entire body quivered with delight in response to the memory, but … with every ray of light, there is always a shadow. I wanted the connection with Austin, the man I loved, but not if it meant we'd become like Malcolm and Maggie. Or was it already too late? Austin had forced me to kill Tasha, the blonde healer, in cold blood. We'd enjoyed her death together … drank down her regrets like sweet ambrosia. And yet today he'd stopped. What was different between Tasha's death and the failed attempt?

"I saw myself in him," Austin's mind whispered to mine. *"His thoughts made me think about you, and how it would be if you were left waiting for me ..."*

My heart fisted. *"His love saved him?"*

"Yeah." A bitter laugh accompanied his reply.

I bit my lip and let my sappy words spill without regard. *"Let my love save you, Austin ... save us. I can save us. You just have to let me."* When he didn't respond, I decided to push the issue. *"We'll protect each other from the darkest parts of death's taint ... Please, Alex. We'll protect each other just like we promised when we were kids."*

"Don't ever fucking use that name again. Alex is dead. Or he might as well be."

Our connection snapped, burning the last remnants of my hope. Did I really think it was going to be that easy?

Curling into a ball, I hugged my knees tightly to my chest. I wasn't certain what it all meant. Austin still loved me, that much I did know. His emotions for me hadn't wavered at all, and yet ... he wanted no reminders of his birth name, Alex. Of course, didn't I feel that Chloe had been buried in a manner of speaking? Absolutely. Chloe was dead, and Samantha was now running the show. Maybe I was simply overcomplicating the situation with Austin? After all, I knew the draw of feeling death emotions and the guilt that accompanied them. The fact that some part of him still felt any guilt at all was a good thing. Some of the actions he'd taken recently caused me to believe otherwise. There were a few gut-wrenching moments when I thought my Austin was completely gone. The relief that he wasn't was palpable. But it wouldn't be long before he disappeared forever, and then his love for me wouldn't be enough. Our story would end as a tragic tale just like so many others before us ... specifically Maggie and Malcolm.

No. I won't let us become like them.

I felt well and truly alone, completely isolated. Most enjoy some solitude, but it's quite another thing to feel so ... apart from the world. As if I could stand on a football field full of people and still be crushed under the weight of the loneliness caused by the situation with Austin. It'd never been this bad before, even when I thought Austin was a figment of my imagination and Nixon was my real husband. Just the idea of losing Austin forever tore a hole in my chest, leaving me dead and broken inside. It left me with a desperation beyond words.

I need to get out of here. I need to find him—to save him—no matter the consequences. Because if I lose him to the abyss for good, I won't be far behind.

"SAM, you need to wake up. Now."

Nixon's agitated voice snapped me to instant awareness. I jerked straight up in bed, instantly ready for a fight. He stood a few feet away, his arms crossed over his chest. "I don't have time to explain, but I need to get you out of here—now."

Adrenaline and hope surged through my system as I jumped to one very big conclusion. "It's Austin. He's come for me." I couldn't help the smile that played across my lips.

"No. It's not him. It's something much worse." Grabbing me by the shoulders, Nixon forced my gaze to meet his, the chocolate depths imploring me to listen. "Please, Sam. I know you don't trust me—"

"You got that fucking right," I spat.

"You have to listen to me. Please."

I snorted and turned my head. "I don't have to do anything."

Nixon let go and backed away from me, letting my body slump back onto the bed. Turning, he slammed his fist into the wall once while muttering under his breath. A few tension-filled moments ticked by before he finally lifted his gaze to meet mine again. "There are things you don't understand, that even I don't. Like I said, I know you don't trust me, but on this, but— Fuck, you're going to have to trust me on this one. Sam, please. I need to get you out of here, and for once I need you not to fight me."

I narrowed my eyes at him. "Please. You actually expect me to fall for your bullshit again? I mean, seriously, how gullible do you think I am? I don't know why you're putting the effort in. At this point, I just kind of assumed you'd drug me and drag me out of her unconscious. Isn't that kind of our thing now?"

Nixon grimaced, frustration pinching his features. "Fine, if that's the way you want it." He reached behind his back, producing another of his seemingly endless supply of syringes. "After all, I wouldn't want to disappoint my woman."

My gaze riveted to the syringe, I bared my teeth,

responding, "I'm not your woman, Nixon. I never have been and never will be. When the hell are you going to get that through that thick skull of yours?"

"Never say never," he muttered, lunging at me.

Sadly, when it came to pure physical dexterity and strength, Nixon would always beat me in spades. Without my mental abilities, I was at a clear disadvantage, especially in the confined space we were currently in. There was no way for me to defend myself and nowhere for me to go. Of course, that didn't mean I would simply give in.

"Don't you dare!" I scrambled backwards on the bed, kicking and flailing as I went.

"We could have done this the easy way." Grabbing my ankle with ease, Nixon pulled me towards him as I kept kicking at him with my free leg.

As I was drawn ever closer to him, I screamed in frustration, clawing and biting at any part of Nixon I could reach. His dark eyes glinted with some unreadable emotion as they met mine a second before the needle plunged into my thigh.

"Fuck you, Nixon! Fuck you, you fuc—"

I fell into darkness.

Chapter 3

Groaning, I moved my head back and forth, the insides having become something akin to cotton candy. When I attempted to move my arms and legs, nothing happened, as if my body wasn't responding to the signals my brain was giving it. Even my eyelids refused to open, the weight of them unnaturally heavy. My thoughts were fragmented, my concentration scattered. I floated in a dreamlike haze, although I was fairly certain I was awake.

A loud explosion lanced through my temples, and I winced but I was unable to lift my hands to my ears for protection. My body was shifted and jostled, Nixon muttering under his breath an impressive string of swearwords.

Time passed oddly, and I realized I was probably slipping in and out of consciousness, the sounds around me changing seemingly instantaneously. Suddenly, all movement stopped.

"No. She was never part of the deal, and I won't let you have her," Nixon growled.

"Change of plans," Cal's familiar voice snapped. "Austin isn't responding quite the way they need him to. She's the key to getting what they want."

"No—"

Darkness pressed down on me, and it was clear I missed part of the conversation when I swam back to the surface of awareness.

"If you leave now, I'll let you live." Nixon's voice vibrated with anger. "But if you try to take her from me, even if you succeed temporarily, I will fucking kill you. Mark my words."

"You can try," Cal retorted with a hint of amusement.

"You think you can best me, you little—"

I plunged into darkness again.

A CALLUSED *hand slid over my mouth and my eyes blinked open to the muted bathroom light casting shadows across our room. I inhaled sharply, relaxing as I picked up on Austin's spicy scent. I grunted, confusion still nettling my sleep-fogged brain. Then I remembered falling asleep on our bed waiting for Austin to get out of the shower.*

"Shhh ..." Austin's hot breath fanned along my neck as he

pressed up behind me. "I'm going to fuck you and I don't want you to make a sound. Do you understand me?"

Oh, so he wants to play. *I nodded, my nostrils flaring as excitement surged. As much fun as it was to dominate Austin, I would be lying if I said I didn't enjoy him taking full control of me more.*

Austin flipped me onto my back and tore my nightshirt from me. I narrowed my eyes at him with a promise of retribution later. I could tell by the sparkle in his baby blues that he'd ruined one of my favorite sleep T-shirts, an oversized one I'd stolen from him, just to get a reaction out of me. Asshole. *I stifled a moan as he dipped his head to suckle my right nipple.* Okay, asshole with a very talented mouth.

"Asshole who happens to be your husband. I said no talking. Love and obey me, wife." *Austin's voice cut into my thoughts, warm with humor.*

"Get out of my mind! Those were thoughts, not talk—" *I couldn't even think the end of my sentence at him as he slid down my body and began to suck on my clit. I bucked against the pull of his mouth, biting my lower lip to keep quiet.*

"I bet you want to obey me now?" *Austin retorted in my mind, chuckling against my over-sensitized flesh, causing me to cry out. He immediately stilled and then sat up on his haunches, a smile ghosting his glistening lips before he furrowed his brows. "Uh-oh ... you seem to have made a sound. A rather loud one after I specifically told you not to." He shook his head slowly. "You know what that means? As your husband, I have the right to punish you as I see fit."*

I rocked my hips up into the air, not wanting to play any

more games. I just wanted him inside me. "Come on, will you just—"

"Fuck you? I was getting there, but then you, my beautiful wife, were disobedient. Now I have to punish her first." Austin lunged at me, flipping me onto my stomach.

Squirming and kicking, I attempted to gain the upper hand. "Stop it! Whatever you're going to do, just stop all the ridiculousness and fuck me!"

He said nothing as he pinned me down to the bed with his strong hands and—bit my left ass cheek. Hard. I screamed and then giggled before renewing my fight. But a moment later his teeth sank into my other cheek, and I screamed again.

"I miss the way it used to be." Austin's voice rolled through my mind.

Wait, what's going on? The last thing I remembered was—

My eyes flew open to pitch-blackness. Disorientated, I panicked, not knowing where I was, or what was going on. Scrambling around on all fours, I searched for some kind of clue—any kind of answer I could find in the darkness. Nothing but cold, hard surfaces met my shaking hands and fingertips. My panic began to paint a picture of me being trapped in a smooth box with no way out, and I fought to breathe normally, my pulse pounding against my eardrums.

Finding a corner, I began to scratch, trying to dig my way out of confinement with my bare hands. A part of my mind screamed at me to stop, to calm down and form a rational plan, and yet I kept clawing in the corner, my chest constricting more with each passing moment as my panic continued to rise in tandem.

I need out. I need out of here now. Please, let me out!

"Let me out of here!" I screeched. "Let me the fuck out!" It was almost complete sensory deprivation. I felt no one's emotions nearby, I couldn't see anything, hear anything beyond my heart pounding and my nails scratching against the unseen surface.

"Let me out!"

I need out! I need the fuck out of here! Please ... let me out! Let me out! Let me out ...

Sobbing, I tore at anything I could reach, but nothing changed or moved. I was trapped ... trapped ... trapped.

Please! Let me out! Let me out! Let me out ...

Minutes, hours, days, I had no clue how long I was there. It felt like an eternity within an eternity.

Please ... please ... please ... Let me out! Let me out! Let me out ...

Finally, exhaustion took hold, and I sagged into myself, curling into a ball. "Austin," I muttered. "Austin, please. Austin, you need to get me out of here. Please."

I had no idea if he could hear me on any level, but I continued with my verbal and mental pleas. I didn't care if it made me seem weak to whoever was holding me captive. None of that mattered anymore as long as I got out, and soon.

Austin, please, you need to get me out. I can't be here. Please, help me. Please, Austin, please ...

Chapter 4
AUSTIN

W*hat the fuck?* I'd been in Sam's mind—connected—when she was torn from me without warning. If it was Nixon and his abilities I would have known. No. It wasn't him. *Something's wrong.* My confusion and panic morphed into blinding rage. *If someone hurt her, they'll die the most painful, wretched kind of death possible.*

"Where the fuck is she?" Dizziness assaulted me as I spun in a tight circle in my cell, tugging at my hair. "I'll fucking kill every last one of you! I'll rip your fucking hearts out with my bare hands!" My pulse thumped inside of my skull almost painfully, my vision muddled by a haze of rage.

Abruptly the small slit on the door slid open and I lurched forward, shoving my arm through as I blindly groped for whoever was on the other side. I'd force them to release me or choke the life out of them in the process. I didn't care much which one as long as the result was me getting to Sam.

My fingers snagged on what felt like a T-shirt, and I curled my fist tightly around the worn material, yanking hard. A loud thud sounded on the outside of the door, a portion of Cal's face now visible to me through the small opening. I slipped into his mind, but before I could dig my claws in, he ejected me with the aid of his ability.

Images of Sam, dead, blood pooling under her motionless body, ripped through my mind. My grip on Cal loosened involuntarily as I staggered back, clutching at my head. I knew what he was doing—that Cal was planting the false pictures in my psyche to manipulate and control me—but just the thought of her like that took me back to the time when I'd believed I lost her for good. *Never again. I won't lose her again.*

"Stop. Fucking stop," I rasped.

"Then back off," Cal choked out.

"I'll back off when you tell me where the fuck she really is and what you've done with her."

"She's unharmed ... for now. But whether or not she stays that way is completely up to you."

I ground my teeth together, fighting to rein in my temper. *Be calm. For her. You can do anything for her.* "What do I need to do?"

Chapter 5
SAM

How long have I been here? Hours, days ... months?

Time had become meaningless, an eternity of pitch-black emptiness laid out before me, no beginning and no end. It was more than the confinement that was getting to me or the absence of light. It was the lack of connection to … anything.

I'd never had enough control to isolate myself completely from the world and all its emotions. My shields always let something sneak past eventually. And when I'd relied on Austin or Nixon to put a wall around me and my abilities, their proximity soothed my anxieties about being cut off and powerless. What I was currently experiencing was something new—something wrong. I couldn't see or feel anything. I was completely and utterly alone in every way imaginable.

I sat on the cold, hard floor rocking back and forth … rocking, rocking, rocking. I was numb, except for my throbbing fingers, the lengths of them covered in the crusty texture of dried blood.

"Austin," I muttered to myself. "Austin, please."

He'd somehow always found a way to reach me before, and the only thing keeping me from completely snapping was the hope that he would this time as well. After all, that's what we did ... we saved each other. No matter the circumstances we could count on each other. I'd always come for him, and he'd always come for me.

But what if that's why I'm here, to keep me from saving him? What if he doesn't even know I need him right now?

A scream erupted from me, raw and bitter, continuing until it felt like it might rupture my lungs. Gasping for breath, I collapsed back onto the floor, sobbing brokenly. Fresh panic surged, my mind reeling as—

I whipped my head around, blinking rapidly as the unmistakable sound of a lock turning pierced the silence, followed by the grind of metal on metal. A thin beam of light streaked through the darkness, and I stood, stumbling forward as if reaching it alone would mean my complete and utter salvation.

I was pulled abruptly into Austin's mind.

Cal's angular face pinched with annoyance as he spoke. "We talked about this, Austin. You want your wife back in one piece then you follow our instructions. For each thing you do, she'll get something to ease her situation."

Austin's anger surged, sweeping through me.

Relief quickly washed away his anger the instant he

became aware of my presence in his mind. *"Sam ... fuck. Sam, are you okay? Talk to me."*

His voice was like a balm to my soul as it rattled through my head. "Austin, I'm …" I paused, attempting to compose myself. I couldn't afford to raise his concern unnecessarily when he needed to focus on saving himself since I wasn't currently in the position to. In the end, I would endure whatever I had to for him. "I'm okay now that I can hear your voice."

Not satisfied with my answer, Austin pushed further into my mind to poke around. After a moment, he growled, *"Those fuckers. I'll kill them."*

His attention snapped back to Cal. "You will be letting her out of there now." Rage simmered within him, welcome to me as opposed to the terror I'd been previously experiencing.

"We've already discussed this. Her well-being all depends on you. Do as you're instructed, and she won't be harmed. Otherwise, we'll be forced to use her as a bargaining chip."

The thin shaft of light abruptly disappeared with a sharp click, along with my connection to Austin. I dropped back to the floor in a heap, sobbing softly. I was exhausted both mentally and physically. I was hungry, thirsty … and there was nothing I could do in my present situation to alleviate any of it.

Wrapping my arms around myself, I began to rock again as I strained my ears, waiting for something else … anything else to happen.

SMILING BROADLY, *I eyed the holes in my target at the gun range. Every single one was a kill shot. I glanced over at Austin while he loaded his clip. His gaze met mine as he smirked. "I'm still a better shot than you."*

I barely resisted the urge to stick my tongue out at him. "No, you're not."

"Care to enter into a wager with me?" One dark eyebrow lifted in challenge.

"What are you, British now? A wager, really?" I paused, nibbling on my lower lip. "Of course, I do," I snapped. "What are we betting?"

"Loser owes the winner a blowjob whenever and wherever he wants."

"Ummm ... Yeah ... I see what you did there, but you're not winning so there will be no blowjobs. I'm thinking your tongue is going to get a workout instead."

Austin chuckled. "We'll see."

"Yes, we will."

Twenty minutes later we were at an impasse. Apparently neither one of us was a better shot than the other. Figured. I wasn't sure what to think about that since my ego was off sulking.

"Come here, my good Sammy girl," Austin commanded, his voice gruff.

"Nope," I grumbled. "You don't get to tell me what to do, you didn't win the bet so no blowjob for you."

"Fuck the bet. Or I guess, fuck you, really, because that's what I'm about to do."

His words didn't have time to register before I was pushed up against the wall, face first. Austin wound one hand around my hair and bowed my neck back for better access. His feverish lips burned a path down my flesh, his other hand sliding down the front of my pants to circle my clit. I moaned in pleasure, arching into him.

My brain warred with my body's desires though. "Not here, Austin, someone could walk in on us."

"Don't care," Austin growled against my skin as he plunged a finger into me.

I ground myself against his hand, all reason fleeing from me. No one would walk in on us, and if they did, they could just turn right around until we were done. I refused to be ashamed of the things I did with my husband—the man I loved. "Oh God, Austin, please."

Austin pulled away from me, leaving me feeling momentarily bereft, but only long enough so he could yank down my pants and his, to plunge his rock-hard cock into me. I cried out with delight as he began to fuck me roughly against the wall. The fingers of his left hand bit into my hip as he gripped my throat with his right hand.

"My good fucking Sammy girl, she always loves it when I take control. Some things will never change." His lust-roughened words elicited another moan from me. My fingers curled against the wall and my body clenched up, reaching—reaching. I screamed, long, loud, and raw as my orgasm ripped through my system.

"I love you, I fuckin' love you," Austin rasped.

"I wish we could go back … I just wish we could go back. It was so much simpler then, at least I thought it was." Austin's words punched into my mind, moving down to stab me in my heart, just as my eyes snapped open.

Chapter 6
NIXON

"Sa-am—" I brokenly croaked.

My throat was cracked and dry, and my eyelids heavy. The last thing I remembered was trying to make our escape when Cal came for Sam.

How many fucking times is the horrible decision of trusting Cal going to bite me on the ass?

The traitor had somehow knocked me out and taken her. I was shocked to find myself still breathing. I had no misgivings that anyone actually cared enough to keep me alive beyond my usefulness. Which meant I still had a role to play in the fucked-up game I couldn't seem to escape. A game I thought I was winning, but as it turned out, I didn't even know what the real stakes were.

"Fuck." My fingers curled against the cool, rough ground, but I couldn't rouse myself to full alertness. My head throbbed, and I was sure there would be a bump the size of a Buick on my skull.

I have to get to Sam—have to get her away—have to hide her from them. I knew they wouldn't kill her, and that fact gave me a bit of comfort. They needed her for leverage with Austin. But they would hurt her. Do whatever they deemed necessary to her in order to control Austin. When I finally got to her, there was no telling what kind of state she would be in.

Sucking in a few ragged breaths, I mustered the willpower to roll onto my back, the small exertion pushing darkness down on me again. *Maybe Cal left me for dead?* There was no way I was going to allow that injustice to happen though. Not when Sam needed me. She was all I'd ever wanted, and I wasn't going to let a little thing like death stand in my way.

Sam's beautiful smile danced within my mind as oblivion won its battle with me.

Chapter 7
SAM

My scream was muffled by a tight gag in my mouth, the stiff material abrading my mouth and tongue. I thrashed against the bindings keeping me attached to a cold metal table, goosebumps erupting along my exposed arms and shoulders. A bright light blazed into my eyes, blinding me. But my connection to Austin was back in place so it wasn't all bad. Whimpering softly, I turned my attention to what was happening with him, ignoring my own tenuous situation.

Austin and Cal were cloaked in the shadows of an alleyway, watching as people strolled by, completely unaware of their presence. Irritation warred with anxiousness within Austin, although a part of him yearned for what Cal was offering.

"Just pick someone so we can get this over with," Austin hissed.

Cal snorted but didn't turn his gaze towards Austin. "You're not fooling anyone. I know you want to kill, so you can stop with the act." When Austin didn't say anything in response, Cal chuckled, a low vibration escaping into the dark. "Tonight is your choice. Just don't try to pick someone who's a criminal or some shit like that so you can rationalize their death. You need to pick someone good if you want to save your wife from ..." His voice trailed off.

Anger swelled within Austin. "From what? Beyond her being isolated in that room." Suddenly he was aware of our connection, and he slipped into my mind to search for details of what was currently happening with me. Fear intermingled with white-hot rage when he realized I was being restrained on a table for some unknown reason.

"What the fuck?" Austin's voice grew louder, his temper barely manageable. "I mean ... What. The. Fuck?" He seemed temporarily incapable of formulating a full, coherent thought.

"Pick someone soon and you won't have to find out," Cal stated blandly.

I hated Cal. He'd played us all for fools and was indirectly responsible for Austin and me being in the situation we were in now. I didn't give a shit anymore what Cal's motivations were. Most likely he hadn't told us the truth anyways.

"No," Austin growled. "Let her go first and then I'll choose."

I immediately paid for Austin's attempt at taking control of the situation. The pinky finger on my left hand was yanked back into an unnatural angle, and my ears registered the snapping sound a split second before my nervous system acknowledged the pain. A muffled scream escaped me, something that wouldn't have happened if I'd been prepared for the physical assault.

Austin's panic surged. *"Sam!"*

As the sharp pain ebbed into a dull ache, I gathered myself and managed to push my response to Austin down our connection. *"I'm fine. It's fine. It's just a broken finger. I've had worse."*

A memory rose to the forefront of my mind completely unbidden.

I whimpered behind a gag as Natalie slapped me across the face. I'd never really been hit before, the shock of it more terrifying than the physical pain itself. I could feel her studying me with cold detachment, like I wasn't even human, like I was some kind of lab rat. She had no real compassion for me.

"Stop!" Alex cried out. "Stop hurting her! I promised I'd protect her! Please!" Alex sounded younger than his actual age, not anything like the stoic protector I'd come to know and depend on.

My scream lodged in my chest when Natalie wrenched my finger to the side, black spots dancing in front of my eyes.

"No! Stop! Please!" Alex yelled, desperation in his tone. "Please! I'll do whatever you want as long as you stop hurting her! Please!"

His voice was the last thing I heard before darkness stole me away.

My attention cut back to the present. Mine and Austin's current predicament was eerily similar. I, again, was being used as leverage to control him. I'd developed a bit more of a pain tolerance over the years though … unfortunately. If I lost consciousness now, I'd not only get a temporary reprieve from the torture, but it would buy some time for the both of us. I was guessing faking being out cold wasn't an option either under the circumstances.

Austin shuffled around in my thoughts, pressing, studying. He wanted as much information as he could possibly glean from me while he had access. He searched for any clues of my whereabouts, faces that I might have seen, any detail, no matter how small that he could use to locate me.

The delay didn't go unnoticed though. My foot was gripped tightly and twisted. White light exploded behind my eyelids, and I thrashed as the excruciating pain burned its way up the nerve endings of my leg, settling in my chest. Sweat intermingled with tears as they both trailed down my face. After what seemed like an eternity, the sensation ebbed into a dull ache, pulsing in time with my broken finger.

Austin's white-hot fury skittered through our connection, causing my physical pain to shift into the background as I strained my focus back on him and Cal.

"Leave her the fuck alone! If you don't, I swear I'll kill you right here and now. And when I'm done, I'll track down every last one of the pieces of shit involved in the loosest sense and I will rip their goddamn intestines out by way of their throats." Spittle flew from Austin's mouth as his fingers tightened around Cal's throat as if he was about to illustrate his threat to him.

"They'll kill her if you don't let me go," Cal choked out, clawing at Austin's forearm.

"No. They wouldn't dare."

"Do it, Austin. Kill him. Kill him and you'll be free."

I was done being the instrument of his destruction. And although I hated the idea of having to sacrifice my life, even for the man I loved, I would do it if it meant he could well and truly be free from torment once and for all. Plus, I knew deep down that we wouldn't get our happily-ever-after anyways. I was already too far gone to be saved, and my death was coming soon one way or another. It might as well be for a noble cause, and there is none nobler than love.

Austin's attention razored in on me. "I won't lose you. I can't. Not again."

Austin's grip loosened on Cal enough for him to rest his feet on the ground. He stepped away from Austin while rubbing his throat gingerly.

"He's not ready," Cal muttered, and suddenly everything went dark.

WHEN I CAME TO, I found myself in my own personal hell again, aka the pitch-black prison room. Vague impressions of Austin and Cal assaulted my mind. I tried to grasp them, sort them out, but they slipped through my metaphorical hands like water.

My finger and toe throbbed, but nothing hurt quite as much as knowing what was happening to Austin because of me. In all honesty, I didn't think whoever was holding me would actually kill me. They needed me to control Austin. I was their ace up the sleeve, and without me, Austin would probably slaughter every single one of them in the most brutal fashion. They had to be aware of the very real threat he would become if he had nothing left to lose. No one with half a brain would risk setting Austin loose in that manner.

Sitting up slowly, I blinked my eyes rapidly in the dark despite being aware of the futility of the action. There was still no light of any kind. Skimming my hands over my body, I was able to ascertain that my finger had been treated with a split, and my toe had been bandaged. After tentatively exploring my foot with my uninjured hand, I came to the conclusion that my big toenail had been ripped off. The fact that my injuries were minor in the grand scheme of things, aligned with my theory of my captors not actually wanting to kill me.

I needed to figure out a way to use that to my advantage. I'd panicked before. Had let my complete isolation and the novelty of it terrify me to my core, but I needed to push past that now.

A plan—a real workable plan. I will come up with one so I can get out of here and save Austin. Before it's too late for him.

Curling into a ball on the floor, I gnawed on my bottom lip.

I'll think of something. After all, I have plenty of time to concentrate with zero distractions.

Chapter 8

SAM

"If only we didn't need her for him to use those powers." Natalie's voice sounded far away. "I was hoping once he experienced them that he would be able to duplicate them, especially since the skill sets are so similar."

"Their powers are intermingling, changing to form something new in both of them. He's able to feel death emotions now without being directly connected to her, but I worry that her death would change that. They always had the strongest bond out of all the pairs. There are aspects of it that we don't understand yet, so we shouldn't risk making an irreversible move at this point," a familiar masculine voice responded.

"I think our biggest mistake was creating the pairs. His love for her anchors him to her morality. If we can corrupt her completely, perhaps he will follow. We'll continue with the conditioning. We'll pick up where we left off. I'm determined to see this to the end. And I grow tired of waiting for the results I know are possible."

"Agreed."

Jolting awake, confusion nettled as I realized I was still in my pitch-black prison and not in a place where I could have overheard the conversation I'd just heard. Or was it a dream? Perhaps a dream of a memory? And if it was a memory, why did my subconscious deem it important now other than the obvious correlation to my present situation?

My stomach gurgled and twisted with hunger, and I pressed my hand over my abdomen. *There's no way I'm going to figure out any of that now with how exhausted and ravenous I am. I'll just have to stick a pin in it like everything else beyond my immediate survival needs.*

My more pressing questions were: Would food be brought to me soon? Or at all? Would my captors afford me any kind of hospitality? Or was I going to starve to death while living in my own squalor? How many days could a person go without food and water? I knew the numbers once, but currently I was coming up with nothing.

How the hell am I supposed to come up with a decent escape plan if I can't even think straight?

I shook my head. *But I have to somehow, despite my physical limitations, because Austin is counting on me. I have to save him, and the clock is ticking.*

Something rough and clammy slid over my mouth, and I thrashed in surprised panic as I somehow registered it was a hand. I dug my nails into a thin forearm while I tried to wrench free.

"Shhh …" a male voice whispered against my ear. "I'm not here to hurt you. I'm a prisoner, too." Several heartbeats passed before he spoke again, "If I take my hand away, will you promise not to scream?"

Sucking in calming breaths through my nostrils, I nodded demonstratively. How the hell had he managed to find my mouth in the dark to cover it to begin with? And somehow remain completely silent in the process to boot?

The hand fell away a moment later, and I whirled in the direction I sensed the intruder was. "Who are you and how the hell did you get in here?"

"I crawled through the ventilation system."

"What? How the—"

"Shhh … I don't want them to hear us. That'll blow any chance we have."

"Okay," I hissed. "I'm just a bit confused." For all I knew this guy could be a plant. Someone for me to trust that would fuck me over at a later date. However, it would be to my benefit to play along. If he was legit, I had nothing to lose, and if he was a fake then I wanted a chance to play him before he did the same to me.

"Do you know where you are?"

"Besides my own personal hell?" I muttered.

A low snort sounded. "Yeah, besides that."

"No, but how about you fill me in since you seem to be such a wealth of information. Also, don't leave out exactly who you are."

"I'm Jake. I would say it's nice to meet you, but under the circumstances, it would be a lie. We're being—"

"What kind of power do you have? Something that enables you to sense in the dark?"

"Power?"

"Yeah, power … or ability. Whatever you want to call it. Tell me what it is."

"I'm a healer."

I ground my teeth together. "Well, that's just great." I didn't exactly have the best history with healers. In fact, the only two I'd ever met were now both dead … because of me. And why couldn't Jake have a more useful power, like lock-picking or something?

Jake's fingers wound around my wrist. I opened my mouth to protest, but my words stalled in my throat when my finger and toe tingled, miraculously feeling better. Okay, maybe not miraculously since I'd seen what a talented healer could do, but it felt like something very special to no longer be hurting. It always did no matter how many times I'd experienced it.

"It is great, isn't it?"

I could hear the challenge in his voice.

"Fine, it's great. But as you were saying. I already know the government has us, but why are you here? I know why I am …" I trailed off as I waited for his response.

"I'm-I'm here because of Cal." Jake's voice wavered slightly. "I'm here because I'm the leverage."

Now that caught my attention. Was Jake to Cal what I was to Austin? "Are you his brother, best friend … what?"

"Best friend, love of his life."

"So you and he …" I cleared my throat. "You and Cal

are a couple?" I was far from uncomfortable when it came to same sex anything, it was just that Cal didn't seem like someone capable of an emotion such as love, let alone romantic love. It made more sense if he had a brotherly or best friend kind of affection, one that was developed in childhood and possibly only upheld through habit.

"Yeah. We met a few years ago in the program, and ... well, things progressed from there."

"The program?"

"The Reaper Program or Project Reaper. I've heard it called both, but it's the same thing. Where they select and take in people with special gifts and condition them to become assassins. You know the drill. It seems like all governments are perpetually looking for an edge to give them more power over everyone else, blabbity blah."

I shoved the sense of dread and foreboding aside for the moment. It wouldn't do me any good to dwell now when I actually had the opportunity to get, hopefully, legitimate information. "And you and Cal volunteered for this program or project, or whatever you want to call it?"

Bitter laughter met my ears. "Hell no. They recruited us, and I'm using that term very loosely."

What was it—more experiments like they did to Austin and me when we'd been kids? That would make sense. At least partially. It seemed like the more questions I got answers to, the more those brought up. "So why are you a prisoner and Cal is out on a mission?"

"You know Cal? Wait. How do you know Cal's out on a mission?"

"Because whoever is running the Reaper Program is using Cal against my husband and me." I ground my teeth together when I thought about everything we'd been through lately.

"I'm sorry."

I swallowed around the sudden lump in my throat. "Not your fault. I can't help but ask though. Cal seemed ... well, he seemed to be enjoying what he did, killing and torturing. Was he always like that or—"

"No!" Jake snapped. "They made him that way. In the end, he wasn't skilled enough for what they ultimately wanted, but his abilities were still useful, so they ... used him. And me."

Sudden light blinded me as the door swung open, thumping against the wall. My eyes focused just in time to see several bulky men dressed in all-black attire resembling SWAT uniforms but missing the actual lettering. They surrounded Jake and restrained him with ease, despite him fighting like some kind of rabid animal. Jumping to my feet, I pummeled the nearest man with my fists and kicked at the back of his knees. No one paid me any mind though since I was too weak at the moment to cause any trouble. I couldn't even muster a mild psychic attack.

Jake was carried out of the room by his legs and arms even as he continued to twist and try to break free. Just before the door was slammed in my face, I got a clear look at my fellow captive in the bright hallway lighting.

His left ear was missing, replaced by ragged scar tissue,

and several of his fingers on each hand were completely missing as well, leaving behind more scarred flesh. And those were just the physical signs of his torture. There was no telling the emotional and mental damage.

They're going to do that to me if I don't get out of here soon.

Staggering back, my gaze lifted to lock with Jake's dark eyes until I was once again encased in pitch-blackness.

Fuck. Why didn't I try to escape while their attention was on Jake?

The door had been wide open.

I crumpled to the floor as I kept my attention on where I knew the door was.

I have to get out of here.

I wasn't exactly the vainest person in the world, but the thought of losing any body part that I was born with or being purposely disfigured was absolutely horrifying.

My fingers involuntarily trailed up to cover my ears.

Shit. I need to get out of here before I end up like Jake. Or worse.

Chapter 9
NIXON

My shaking hands clenched into fists as rage replaced terror. *No. No, I won't let it happen. I'll find a way. I have to find a way.*

But the truth of my vision was undeniable. I'd seen Sam, my Sam, dying in my arms.

I slammed my fist into the wall. I wouldn't accept it. I couldn't. Nothing I saw was ever a certainty, a one hundred percent guarantee. It simply meant if the people involved continued down their current path, then the event I foresaw would come true.

So, I simply wouldn't let it happen. I would get to her. Change the trajectory of … everything. I would save her.

Somehow.

Someway.

Chapter 10
SAM

My mouth opened wide, a ragged scream rushing out.

My hand, my right hand, was missing the last two digits. They were gone. Just gone. The skin was smooth with no scars as if I'd never had a complete hand at all. Had I been healed? How long since they'd been taken?

My heart thrashed against my ribcage as I lifted my mangled hand to my right ear. I stopped breathing, the air lodging in my throat.

Nothing.

There was nothing there.

They'd done it—taken my fingers and ear just like they'd done to Jake.

My lungs burned as I finally sucked in oxygen, my entire body shaking uncontrollably. Had they done anything else? I was petrified to check, and yet not knowing was worse. Although …

My gaze snagged on where my right leg should have been—

My scream erupted around me in the darkness, and I pitched to the side from my sitting position, landing in a heap on the ground. My hands flew over all of my fingers, my ears, my legs, checking and assessing. Only when I verified that everything was still intact did I allow myself to relax a bit.

It was just a nightmare. Obviously triggered by seeing what was done to Jake earlier.

But it could become a reality. At any time.

Those were the worst kind of nightmares. The ones where you can't assure yourself of their ridiculousness when you wake up. The best you could do was tell yourself that it hadn't happened … yet, and that there was still time to prevent the horrifying events from taking place. Hopefully.

A click and a scrape, metal upon metal, snagged my attention as a previously unseen mini-door opened at the bottom of the normal-sized one. A thin band of light streamed through as a covered plate and several water bottles were shoved through the opening.

I dove for the water, grabbing hold of a bottle before the door was shut, taking the light with it. After chugging all of the contents, I felt around for the plate, uncovering what smelled like food. I didn't quite register what I was eating as I shoved it into my mouth with my hands, only chewing enough so I didn't choke. In the end, it wouldn't have mattered, I was ravenous enough to not have cared.

Nausea roiled my gut, and I curled into a ball, praying I was able to keep the food and water down. Eating and drinking at such a pace after having nothing for so long was a monumental mistake, one I hoped I didn't suffer for.

Exhaustion took hold, a huge yawn cracking my jaw as sleep crept in to steal me away.

LOUD VOICES JOLTED me into instant awareness, although I couldn't make out what anyone was saying. Bright colors exploded around me, my vision blurry, my confusion quickly turning to panic.

Then everything splintered as pain dug its wretched claws into every molecule of my body. The agony—the agony went beyond words, beyond my scope of understanding. I was being broken into a billion pieces. I was shattering, being unmade …

Wetness coursed down my cheeks, blood or tears, I wasn't sure which. Maybe both. Not that it mattered. Nothing mattered anymore except escaping the pain.

And then it stopped.

I floated in a euphoric state, a type of limbo created simply by the absence of pain.

Images slammed into me, as if they were implanted directly into my brain. Men, women, children all in various stages of decomposition or dying. It was bloody and beyond horrific.

I breathed a sigh of relief when those too ceased. But my reprieve was short-lived. My body was again consumed in pain, if that word could even begin to describe what was happening to me. It seemed to last longer the second time around … my agony. The euphoric state that followed was much more intense, and so were the mental pictures.

And so it went … agony, euphoria, and death … agony, euphoria, and death … over and over until I lost all concept of anything beyond those things.

I'd been under the impression that what Malcolm had done to me was torture, or what David and Natalie had put me through when I was no more than a child. I no longer believed those falsehoods. I'd never known true torture until now.

I prayed—the almost foreign syllables spilling from lips that I wasn't sure existed anymore. But I knew no one could help me. I was at the mercy of my tormentors.

I would give them whatever they wanted to make what they were doing to me stop. Finally, when I spoke those words, or communicated them somehow … when I promised to do whatever they wanted, whatever it was, it all abruptly came to an end.

Darkness swallowed me whole.

"KILL HIM. KILL JAKE." The gentle command settled into my brain.

I remained immobile as I processed the words, not sure if I truly understood them.

"The next time you see Jake, you will kill him. And you will enjoy it."

My head wobbled on my shoulders. "No," I croaked.

A scream was torn from my raw throat as the now familiar pain tore through my nervous system. It went on for an eternity, no ending in sight. But somewhere within the depths of my being, my need to survive latched onto the concept of what they wanted—what I had to do for them. "I'll kill him. I'll kill Jake. Please. I'll do it."

Immediately, a blissful absence of pain cocooned me, the fog of it settling in.

Weak. I'm weak. Austin would be stronger than me in this position. He would win. He would have a plan. I need him. I need my husband. Austin, please.

A sob broke free from my chest. *No, I'm the one who's supposed to save him. I need to save him. I can't let him down.*

Another sob rattled my chest. *I've already let him down. It's too late because I've failed him already. Because I'm not strong enough. I've never been strong enough.*

Chapter 11

SAM

"Samantha, kill it."

"Nooo ..." I wailed, snot running down my face.

In front of me, in a small wire cage, was a black and white floppy-eared bunny. It was so tiny it could have fit in the palm of my hand. Its tiny pink nose twitched at me.

"I can't." I bit down on my lower lip so hard I tasted the coppery tang of my blood. "And why do you keep calling me Samantha? My name," I choked out, "is Chloe."

"She needs more time," Natalie stated blandly.

I couldn't look at her. I hated her. Instead, I reached for Alex, and he slipped into my mind. "Chloe. It's okay. I'm here." *His presence soothed and warmed me. I was still distraught, but everything seemed tolerable when he was connected to me in any way. They tried to separate us, at least temporarily, but the fact that we spoke to each other telepathically was our little secret.*

Pain shot through my system. I dropped to the ground,

curling into a little ball, trying to escape it. Uncontrollable sobs wracked my body when the torture ebbed. I was yanked to my feet and forced to face the bunny again.

"Kill it, Samantha."

Alex's voice faded into the recesses of my mind, hidden and locked behind a barrier. Chloe remained with him. What I needed to do to stop hurting was up to me ... Samantha. I'd chosen my own name. Samantha was strong. She did what needed to be done to survive. Chloe was weak and couldn't handle it.

I unlatched the door to the cage, slid my small hands inside, and snapped the neck of the bunny. I didn't even flinch. I could hear Chloe screaming in horror though. I told her to be quiet, that she needed me to handle this part and she would need me in the future to do the things she couldn't but had no choice to. I don't think she heard me.

I gasped, my heart threatening to pound out of my chest. I was back in my cell. I was beginning to feel like I was in some twisted version of my own *Groundhog Day*. Every time I passed out, I'd wake up back in that damned room.

Pressing the fleshy part of my palms into my closed eyes, I rubbed, groaning. What exactly had I just dreamt? I thought all my memories, even the hidden ones from my childhood, had been returned to me. What I'd just seen was definitely a memory ... A very real, extremely disturbing one. Why hadn't I remembered it before? And I thought Samantha was the name I picked when I was older. I picked it because of Austin. I even remember explaining my reasoning to him, much to my embarrassment.

"WHY SAMANTHA BEVANS?" *Austin's deep voice murmured. "Why choose that name for your new identity? After all this time I never thought to ask you until now."*

"I don't know ..." I said. "I picked the name when I was still trying to convince myself that I hated you. I didn't realize until later, but my subconscious was trying to call me on my bullshit, obviously." I laughed. "When I was a little girl, my mom used to watch Days of Our Lives. *There was a character on the show who was obsessed with this guy named Austin. I don't remember the rest. I was just a kid, and it was a soap opera, so it was kind of confusing to me, but somehow I guess my subconscious just thought, I don't know, her name was Samantha, but they called her Sammy for short. You think it's stupid, don't you?"*

I SCREAMED OUT IN FRUSTRATION. Every single time I thought I had all the information, I became privy to something else—something new, and always more disturbing than the last. Did I still have some false memories or ideas? All the talk of conditioning and the torture I'd suffered both in my childhood and recently ... were my tormentors trying to force some kind of split personality? I'd heard of those types of psychological experiments being done before, but it didn't quite add up. I'd picked my name, I never lost huge chunks of time. In fact, up until the memory I'd just seen, I never had any symptoms of that particular disorder. I probably had a half dozen others, but not a split personality of any kind. And what would be the purpose?

My mind backtracked to the conversation I'd heard where Natalie had mentioned pairs … something niggled at my consciousness. I pushed it aside.

"What would be the purpose? That's a stupid question," I muttered to myself.

I could actually think of quite a few reasons why having me shard off into split personalities would aid the powers that be in reaching their ultimate goals. If Natalie and David had begun this process when we were only children, then maybe …

I bit my lip and uttered my sappy words without regard. "Let my love save you, Austin ... save us. I can save us. You just have to let me." When he didn't respond, I decided to push the issue. "We'll protect each other from the taint. Please, Alex. We'll protect each other just like we promised when we were kids."

"Don't ever fucking use that name again. Alex is dead. Or he might as well be."

Was it already happening to Austin? Was that the real reason why he'd become so angry when I'd called him Alex? Was he losing a part of himself, becoming Austin like I'd been Samantha? And if so, then why did he still love me? *Because all of him loves you, just like all of you loves him,* my mind supplied. It was true. Every part of me, every single molecule of my being, even the darkest parts, loved Austin. No matter what he did or what he'd become,

I'd always love him, and I knew it was the same for him when it came to me. We were connected, bonded in a way that defied logic. If that wasn't the case, I wouldn't be in my current predicament—being held as leverage to force Austin into compliance.

The door to my prison swung open, the heavy door banging into the wall. I forced my aching body to spring to its feet, beating it into submission with my mind, determined not to miss another opportunity to escape. *Mind over matter. I can—no, I will do this.*

With surprising ease, I managed to push my way past the two men in padding and gear. I headed to the right, fleeing like a wild animal, having no idea where I was going but knowing that I needed out.

Despite my determination, my body was weak, and I stumbled, one of the men grabbing me from behind around the waist. I hit the back of my skull into his nose, one of the only unprotected areas on him, the crunch of bone music to my ears. He bellowed, his hands falling away.

Whirling around, I managed to snag what looked like a taser from his belt. Without hesitation, I pointed and pressed the button. Electricity shot across the top between two prongs, and I rammed them to the side of the man's face. He dropped like a bag of rocks.

The second man approached me a bit more warily. We circled each other in a sort of dance, attacker and attackee. The question was, who was going to end up as which? Impatience taking over, he finally lunged at me, and I pressed the prongs under his jaw, dropping him alongside his twitching sidekick. From him I snagged a ring with a key on it.

Swaying slightly, I eyed the row of doors all similar to the one I'd just escaped from. It was time to see who exactly was being kept under lock and key in this hellhole.

I unlocked the door closest to me, and it creaked open ominously as I pushed it open with my toes. Following a groan, Jake ambled into the light, blinking rapidly as his eyes adjusted to the bright light.

A sudden unexplainable urge to wrap my hands around Jake's neck pressed at me and I trembled violently. My mind grasped at a vague memory from my recent torture session, but I couldn't conjure the details. Resisting the violent compulsion directed at Jake, I dashed to the next door.

When the occupant stepped into view, the keys slipped from my fingers, clattering to the ground. "Nixon," I gasped. He'd been locked up next to me the entire time? Or was he a newer acquisition?

His fathomless gaze captured mine as he bared his teeth. "Perfect." Before I had a chance to react, Nixon ripped the taser from my grasp and threw me over his shoulder.

"You've got to fucking be kidding me," I growled. "Put me the fuck down, Nixon. You're not getting away with abducting me—again." I pounded my fists against his back in a familiar effort in futility against him.

Not listening, he took off with me at a sprint. "You

know there aren't such things as coincidences, Sam. Somehow you escaped and ended up opening my door." Nixon's voice was scratchy, and he was out of breath from the small amount of exertion. Apparently, our captors hadn't been treating him much better than their other guests. "I'm getting you the hell out of Dodge like I originally planned. At least now I know I can't trust anyone."

"I'm not going anywhere with you," I grated.

At least this time I didn't have to worry about him sticking me with a syringe full of drugs, unless he really did conjure them from thin air. Pummeling my fists against him, I focused all of my remaining energy on fighting him, not that it made a difference. I might as well have been a flea buzzing around his head for the amount of good it did me.

"What's your ability?" Nixon asked, I was assuming Jake.

"I'm a healer."

"Good." Nixon dropped me onto my feet, dizziness assaulting me at the abrupt movement.

I met his determined gaze just as his fist registered in my peripheral vision.

Chapter 12
SAM

Alex sat on the edge of my bed, pulling me into him so my head came to rest on his shoulder as he wrapped an arm tightly around me. "Chloe, you need to eat something."

"Not hungry," I croaked. An image of my latest atrocity slammed into me, and bile surged up my esophagus. I'd been forced to hurt a puppy with just my mind ... or rather Samantha had. I'd just been there in the front row for the show, forced to witness every gruesome detail.

"It's not your fault. None of it is. You can't help what happens when they—"

"Force me to hurt innocent creatures? Puppies, bunnies, kittens? I can't, I just can't—" Tears burned a salty trail down my cheeks, my body quivering with shame and guilt.

"They can't keep us here forever. Eventually, they'll have to let us go home. Probably soon."

I desperately wanted to believe Alex, but his words weren't based in fact and were only wishful thinking on his part. Not that I didn't appreciate the effort he put in to soothe me. After all, I would have completely shattered a long time ago if it wasn't for him. It was a small comfort knowing he relied on me in the same manner, the two of us keeping each other sane in an insane environment.

But today I didn't have it in me to play along. "Tomorrow is my thirteenth birthday, Alex. We've been here for seven years already."

His fingers curled under my chin as he tipped my face up to meet his gaze. He frowned slightly as he studied me, pausing to swipe at my tears. "You're growing up right before my eyes."

A pleased smile twitched the corners of my lips. An instant crush had bloomed for Alex when I'd first laid eyes on him at the tender age of six. Now my feelings were changing into something I wasn't quite sure of. He was a few years older than me, and just looking at him, having him touch me, made things flutter inside of me. I never dared that he thought of me as something more, convinced he saw me as someone akin to a little sister. Still ... I felt emboldened by his comment. Maybe he could see me as someone more mature, like him, someone he'd want to—

"I want you to be my first kiss," I blurted out.

His eyes widened with surprise. "Chloe, I—"

My cheeks heated with embarrassment. "Never mind. You don't have to. I know you don't think of me like that. I just—"

Alex pressed his index finger against my lips to quiet me. "I'm older than you, Chloe. You don't understand, wouldn't understand the kinds of things I think about. I'm not even sure I do sometimes." He swallowed thickly and glanced away. "I would never ... I could never— You're too young."

"You're not much older than me, not enough that it matters," I said around his finger.

"I can't kiss you now, Chloe. Even if I want to." He frowned at me. "I won't be your first kiss." I opened my mouth to protest again, but a sudden smile lit up his face. "But I'll be your last."

"You will?" Alex got visions or just knew things sometimes. I wondered if he knew something more about our future together. Or maybe he simply wanted to shut me up about it?

He moved his hand so he could cup my cheek. Butterflies did somersaults in my stomach as I lost myself in the depths of his beautiful blue eyes.

He nodded slowly without looking away from me. "Yes. I will."

I beamed up at him, and he blinked as if I had temporarily blinded him.

Pulling away, he cleared his throat. "But not if you don't eat something. If—"

He staggered out of bed, dropping to his knees, and clutched his head. "No, no, nooo!"

"Alex, what is it?" I quickly bent down next to him.

"My mom. I saw— I have to stop it. And—"

He swung his gaze up to meet mine once more. His pupils dilated and then he crumpled to the floor.

I swam to consciousness slowly, not wanting to face the current reality of my life. A life without Austin, and no clear plan on how to get him back before he was forced to succumb to his conditioning.

The more I considered my situation the bleaker everything seemed. It had been Austin and me against the world for as far back as I could remember, and yet now, with our separation, it felt an awful lot like it was me alone against the world. With how far gone Austin was with his death addiction, mere hours, possibly minutes, could make the difference between saving him or not.

I'd been experimented on and conditioned as a child. In ways that quite possibly altered my mind and body beyond my comprehension. How could I be sure any of my thoughts or actions were one hundred percent my own? What if I was still being controlled and I didn't realize it? Just the idea of that made me feel like a caged animal.

I'm trapped, trapped, trapped. Panic swelled within me. *I just need to get to Austin.* I had to focus on getting to him. Nothing else mattered before, or probably after.

"Good. You're awake. You need to eat something."

I squinted up at Nixon, who was hovering near me, his dark eyes roaming my features with concern.

When I tried to rise, I registered something holding me in place, and I warily glanced down. "You can't be serious right now." I was strapped to a bed with padded leather restraints, the kind you might see in a mental facility. I quickly scanned my surroundings. Small, dimly lit room, two doors, nightstand, TV, and Nixon … of course.

I narrowed my eyes at him, wishing I could attack him mentally. "Where do you find these places? Seriously. Is there some kind of special real estate rental guide for would-be kidnappers? Small, clean, soundproof. We don't ask questions. Cash only. Available immediately." I sniggered, exhaustion making me borderline hysterical.

A knock sounded at the door, and Nixon slid cautiously over to peek out through the peephole, before undoing the locks. I got a glimpse of the hallway, and it seemed to be inside a house of some sort, not an apartment. I filed that information away for later in case I needed it, no matter how doubtful it would make any kind of difference.

In stepped Jake, carrying a first aid kit. It was the first time I'd gotten to study him. He had short-cropped brown hair, high cheekbones, and a chiseled jawline. Despite the mutilation of his ear and fingers, he was still very attractive.

Ignoring me for the moment, Jake headed straight for Nixon. "Let me see it."

Nixon lifted his black T-shirt to reveal a deep gash in his side. It was still oozing blood. The sight of it caused me to suck in a sharp breath through my teeth.

"Well, it's good to know that you still care if I live or die," Nixon grated, and then swore under his breath as Jake swiped a cotton pad with antiseptic over the wound.

I ignored his sarcasm. "Why are you not using your healing powers on him? He could have bled out. And by the way, what happened?"

Nixon grunted. "He did use his healing powers. He's just not up to full strength at the moment. He was able to keep me from bleeding out, so I'd probably be dead right now if not for him. I'll have to do the rest on my own or wait for him to get back up to full strength again. Whichever comes first."

"What happened? You were fine when we escaped, weren't you?"

Nixon shifted uncomfortably, and Jake studiously ignored me. Which was odd since we'd sort of been friends before … or at least bonded over being held captive by the same people. Maybe bonded was too strong of a word, but he at least knew me and I let him out of his damn cell so he could escape. He could at least acknowledge my presence.

"What happened, Nixon?" I growled. We'd been fake married for a long time, and I knew when he was hiding something from me.

"You really don't want to know," he mumbled. Jake finished up by slapping on a big adhesive bandage, causing Nixon to wince again. "Thanks, man. You saved my life." He gave Jake a wan smile.

"You saved mine."

"So what are you planning on doing now?" Nixon addressed Jake, the two of them seemingly content to ignore me.

"I need to find Cal," Jake stated. His tone carried the same kind of determination that I heard in my own voice when I said that about Austin.

Nixon grimaced. "You probably shouldn't."

"I love him, so I don't have a choice." Jake turned,

revealing red, angry marks around his neck. It looked as if someone had tried to strangle him…

A memory flashed across my mind.

My fingers tightened around Jake's neck. Nixon struggled to pull me off of him. When Nixon managed to tug me free, I snagged a Swiss Army knife off the nearby table and—

"No." I shook my head slowly back and forth against the bed. "No. Please tell me—" But I knew instinctively it was true. I'd tried to kill Jake and nearly managed to do in Nixon in the process. I had a special kind of dislike for the man who'd kept me from Austin all those years and pretended to be my husband, but I didn't want to see him dead, especially not by my hand. "Wha— Why? I don't understand."

Now I knew why I was being restrained and why Jake was avoiding eye contact with me. "Why would I do that?" I had a sinking feeling in the pit of my stomach, but I was in hardcore denial mode. I swallowed repeatedly to try and dislodge the boulder in my throat. "Jake, you have to know I'm sorry. And Nixon—"

Jake met my eyes with sadness. "I know it wasn't your fault. They did it. Just like everything else."

Nixon tilted his head to study Jake. "Who is *they*, now? David's dead. Natalie's missing. I thought I knew the score, I thought I knew—" He ran his hands through his hair and tugged. "I don't have a fucking clue, do I?"

Jake's lips pressed into a thin line. "I'm not sure anyone knows what's really going on anymore. That's what happens when there are too many secrets.

Eventually, no one knows what anyone else is doing and it becomes—"

"A disaster," I murmured. "A complete and utter disaster."

The three of us were silent for a moment, probably all thinking of how much we'd suffered, the things we'd lost —and the things yet to lose. How did any of us move on when we kept getting fucked over by people with agendas we didn't know about?

A few more moments passed before my mind snapped back to its current default setting. "I need to get to Austin. Please, Nixon, before it's too late."

Nixon's eyes sparked with anger as he clenched his jaw. "Not happening." He turned to Jake in clear dismissal of the subject. "I won't stop you, but again, I don't think you should go after Cal."

Jake raised his hand to silence Nixon. The two of them stared at each other for a long moment. "I don't have a choice. And maybe if I do find him, we can put an end to all of this."

Nixon shook his head slowly. "Good luck then. And I guess this means we'll probably never see you again. I'm taking her and going into hiding."

Arching against my restraints, I spat, "Hell fucking no. We're not doing this again. You can't just keep taking me places against my will." Except that's exactly what he kept doing and I had yet to figure out a way to actually stop him.

Jake glanced at me, sympathy streaking through his

eyes. "Maybe …" He nibbled his bottom lip. "Maybe you should let her find Austin. I know you care about her, but —" His gaze flicked briefly to me again. "I understand the bond. I'm connected to Cal the same way she is to Austin."

Nixon scowled at Jake. "It's time for you to leave."

"Jake, no—please. You can't let him take me from Austin. Imagine if someone kept you away from Cal in the same way. Please, Jake." I writhed against my restraints, imploring Jake with my eyes to help me.

"Get out," Nixon grated. "You may have saved my life, but if you try to take her from me, you'll regret that decision for the rest of your very short life."

Shoulders slumping inward, Jake muttered, "I'm sorry," as he fumbled for the door and slunk away as soon as it was ajar.

Fresh dread settled over me like a familiar blanket. *No, stop. Don't panic. Panic leads to rash decisions, and you've fallen prey to enough of those lately.* I needed to remain calm and focused so I wouldn't miss my opportunity to escape when the time came.

"I hate you," I hissed, unable to resist voicing the sentiment to Nixon.

"Not for long you won't. We're going to go back to the way it was before, Sam. We're going to be happily married and you won't die like I saw—you won't."

No. Not again. The panic I'd been holding back broke free, crashing over me in a violent wave, and my body began to shake uncontrollably. "Nixon, please. Don't do this."

"Shhh … It'll be okay. I have a plan. I have a plan and it has to work." He produced a needle from behind his back, and I inhaled sharply.

With me tethered to the bed, Nixon slid the needle into my arm with ease. He then leaned down to press a kiss to my forehead as my vision dimmed and my thoughts scattered, leaving me to float in oblivion.

Chapter 13
SAM

I stood at a bus stop. The small glass enclosure with the bench was stuffed with people, so I hovered awkwardly just outside. It was a ridiculously hot day, and the afternoon sun beat down on my overheated skin. Sweat dribbled down my spine, and gathered around my hairline, my clothes sticking to my body in random places.

I glanced to my right, squinting, and noticed another enclosure identical to the one I was next to, a little way down the road. It was empty, offering a bit of shade and a chance to rest my legs. Without another thought, I walked over to it and sat down, heaving a sigh of relief.

No sooner had I settled in, than a loud screeching sound filled the air. Lifting my gaze, I spotted a UPS truck, out of control, and barreling down the steep hill overlooking the bus stop where I'd just been. The truck careened down the deep slope and lifted when it lurched over the crest towards the bottom. It was suddenly airborne and headed straight for the people who didn't have time to get out of the way.

The impact caused an explosion, one that rained glass and debris down on me. Lurching to my feet, I fled in a panic. Screams thickened the air, and as I ran, people clamored around me, the same thing on their minds—to put as much distance between the bus stop and themselves as possible.

People were on fire, bleeding. I was the only one who was relatively unscathed. Without slowing my pace, I flicked my gaze over to a man who had smoldering pieces of burnt flesh hanging from his bones. He was something straight out of a horror movie. I shuddered with revulsion. Suddenly, he was much too close to me—

"Fifteen," his hoarse voice said, inside and outside of my head at the same time.

My world tilted, spinning out of control, and I opened my mouth to scream.

"Fuck," I muttered, struggling to pull myself out of the nightmare I'd just been having. I was lying on my back in a dark room. I ran my fingertips tentatively over my arms in an attempt to warm away the goosebumps. That's when I realized that I was no longer being restrained.

"Don't bother. There's a reason I don't need to have you tied to your bed anymore," Nixon rumbled.

I swung my head in the direction his voice had just come from. "Where are we?"

"Doesn't matter. Go back to sleep. You need rest."

"No, I have to—"

"Fifteen," he snapped, interrupting me before I could finish my plea about having to find Austin.

"What?" A chill crept up my spine.

"Fifteen," Nixon repeated, his voice closer to me than it'd just been a moment ago. Then he was whispering in my ear, "Fifteen."

Blinking rapidly, I tried to figure out what the hell was going on and why he kept saying the same thing I'd heard at the end of my nightmare. "Nixon—"

"Fifteen!" he yelled, his hot breath fanning the side of my face.

His voice caused my ears to ring, and I cringed.

"I don't understand!" I screamed back.

I jerked awake, hopefully for real this time. "What the fuck?" I cried out.

I was back in my own personal hell … the pitch-black cell. Had the entire thing been a dream? Or had we all been captured again? I was confused. More than that, my sense of reality was shaken. What I'd felt before was so real—so was it a hallucination, a dream, or truth? Or was now the falsehood?

The only thing that made me question the escape with Nixon was the fact that I'd had no connection with Austin. I'd thought Nixon had something to do with that because of his void power, but the more I thought about it—

"Fuck!" I screamed, grinding my teeth together in frustration.

I really had lost all sense of reality. Was that a result of the conditioning? Or did any of that even happen? Maybe I was some completely insane person with no powers, and Austin wasn't even real. Maybe I was in a padded cell right now and everything else was one big delusion. Maybe … maybe …

No! I could be insane. I can't rule out that possibility, but if I'm not, then sitting here doing nothing isn't going to do me any good. I had nothing to lose if I was certifiable, and everything to lose if someone just wanted me to think I was.

I was being broken down systematically. I was being made to doubt my own reality so another one could be substituted. And the nightmare I'd just had, it meant something … something vital. I could feel it. I needed to figure out what exactly it meant, and I needed to escape in actuality, not just my mind.

Not knowing what was real and what was fiction wasn't something that I was unfamiliar with. *I can handle this.* I just had to work with what I did know to be fact. I knew I was awake, and I knew I was currently in the cell that was keeping me cut off from Austin, and everyone and everything else for that matter. I also knew that I'd had a meal recently since my stomach was no longer trying to eat itself for sustenance. Everything else … I had to file into the uncertain category.

Chapter 14

AUSTIN

I prowled the small hotel room like a caged animal. Which is exactly what I was. My emotions were raw and exposed. I could only think about two things: Sam and death. Having her with me to experience the latter would be the optimal situation. The few times we'd drunken down death emotions together and fucked afterwards was the closest thing to bliss I could imagine. I needed her. I thought I'd be able to keep her safe and away from me now that I'd been tainted like Malcolm. I'd been wrong. And yet . . .

Killing an innocent person with my bare hands, I wasn't sure I could go through with it.

Cal stepped out of the tiny bathroom with nothing but a towel wrapped around his lanky body, his gaze blatantly roaming over me. I ground my teeth together and clenched my fists. "Take a picture, it'll last longer."

Cal smirked. "You going to shower?"

Ignoring his question and follow-up leer, I stated, "I'll do what you guys want—I'll kill an innocent. Just let Sam go and bring her to me. Sam and I will do it together."

"She's our leverage, we can't do that."

"You won't need leverage. You know I'm already too far gone, and she's hanging on by a fingernail. Just—" I struggled to remain calm, knowing bad things had a tendency to happen when I lost control of my emotions. If I inadvertently injured Cal with my mind, like I'd killed Jessica, Sam was as good as dead. "Just bring her to me. I need her."

"I don't think that's true." Cal dropped his towel and slowly walked over to his bag to get dressed; I flicked my gaze away. "You don't really need her at all."

Cal's appearance morphed into Sam's. I knew it wasn't real, Cal couldn't physically shift his body, but his illusions were flawless, making me see exactly what he wanted me to.

"What the fuck?" I muttered, stumbling backwards. Having been deprived for so long, I couldn't help but react to the image of my very naked wife in front of me, reality or not. My dick was instantly rock hard.

"I think you have everything you need right here." Cal even had Sam's voice spot on, the soft tone music to my ears.

"No. It's not real," I mumbled as I continued to back up until I hit the wall behind me. I swiped my hand down my face but couldn't force myself to look away.

"If this body is what you want, I can give it to you."

Sam's big eyes stared up at me as her soft fingertips brushed my arm. "Touch me, Austin. Or," she dropped to her knees, "I can touch you."

Sam unbuckled my belt, and I swallowed hard. Confusion pushed at me, and for a moment, I couldn't remember why I was so angry. My wife … the woman I loved, wanted to wrap her supple lips around my cock. Why would I deny myself that? I loved getting head from Sam. No one had ever done it better.

"Mmmm … that's right, baby, let me take care of you," Sam cooed.

No. It's not my Sammy! "Get the fuck away from me!" The rage coiled within my mind erupted, slamming into Cal. He fell to the floor, his Sam disguise instantly gone as he cried out in pain. I stared down at him, struggling to rein in my emotions.

I knew in that instant, that even if I played the game, Cal would fuck Sam and me over. Plucking the information from him while he was unguarded was simple. Cal wanted Sam gone. He'd loved someone named Jake once, but the pain of his torture had twisted him to where he was desperately seeking someone else—a replacement of sorts. I was the new object of his infatuation. But it wasn't really me he wanted. He ultimately craved freedom, and being attached to Jake was just one more shackle. Cal's emotions were mangled to the point where he couldn't see clearly anymore. If he didn't want to hurt Sam, I might have actually felt sorry for what he went through.

My head whipped up as the front door to the hotel room burst open. One of the last people I expected to see stood on the threshold … Nixon. I froze, the surprise of him rendering me immobile.

Cal groaned, stretching towards Nixon. "Help me," he rasped.

Nixon didn't dignify him with even a wayward glance. His dark gaze was focused solely on me. "We need to get her out. Before it's too late."

I didn't have to ask who he was talking about. Nixon's single-minded obsession with my wife never seemed to diminish. "As if I'd trust you ever again," I grated.

"You don't have to trust me. If we don't get her out soon, she'll die."

Fear punched me in the gut. "You saw it?"

He nodded once sharply. "I saw him, too." Nixon finally acknowledged Cal who was still writhing on the floor. "He has to die. Besides, keeping him alive isn't going to do us any good as a bargaining chip since they only seem to care about you. He's just going to be a liability if we let him live."

"No!" Cal wailed. "I can help! Let me help!"

I sneered. "Sorry. You aren't any good to us alive." I dropped to my knees, leaning over him. "And haven't you been pushing me to kill? Maybe you should have thought that plan out a bit more."

Wrapping my hands around his neck, my lips stretched into a grin. "I'm definitely going to enjoy this."

Cal's eyes widened, going wild. He grasped for his

abilities, but unfortunately for him, his body was too weak from my mental attack.

As I tightened my fingers, I dove into his mind. All his regrets and anguish washed over me like a balm, soothing my nerves. His was the perfect death to enjoy. The unexpected kind usually were. Sam had taught me that. I automatically reached out to try and connect with her. Frustration warred with my temporary bliss.

I need you with me, Sam. Cal's death would have been that much sweeter if Sam—my Sammy girl—could revel in it with me. I was trying to pay attention to the information I was gleaning though, and it was the second thing that was preventing me from enjoying myself fully. I needed to know how to get to Sam. I needed to know—

My gaze swung up to meet Nixon's as I let go of Cal's lifeless body. "I can't believe none of us ever figured it out."

"Now you know."

I barked a humorless laugh. "Yep, now I know that Natalie and David are your parents. Or should I say that David was your father? You didn't even flinch when I shot him."

"He was going to hurt Sam."

"So that's how you were accepted so easily onto David's team and then back onto Natalie's. And why when Natalie went missing you were left in charge. The special treatment all makes sense now."

"Special treatment?" Nixon snarled. "I was tortured by

my own parents. I was right there with all of you in that facility … longer in fact."

That finally answered the lingering questions of what kind of people Natalie and David were, and how far they would truly go to reach their goals. If Nixon hadn't stolen Sam from me, I would have felt sympathy for him. But those kinds of sentiments were buried beneath his betrayal. "Why don't they give you Sam back? Can't you just get Natalie, your mother, to—"

"Her plans are more important than me or what I want, as always," Nixon interjected. "My mother and the rest of her wackjob colleagues want you. Sam can get you for them. What I want doesn't trump that. The best I could hope for is after they have you that they'd give me Sam." He ran his hands through his hair, tugging angrily. "She'll be beyond broken by then, and even I won't be able to fix her." His eyes darkened. "And then she'll be dead." He stalked closer to me. "Look. We hate each other. We both love the same woman. We can go back to hating each other after we save her."

He was right, and I knew it. "Fine. But just remember this … we might both love her, but she only loves me back." I grinned at Nixon as I pushed past him.

It was going to be extremely difficult to not kill him even if it was only until we rescued Sam.

Chapter 15

NIXON

I knew exactly where I was being held. And the fact that I was in the same building as Sam, both enraged and sickened me. It'd been a long time since I felt so utterly helpless, the unwanted nostalgia taking me back to when I was just another name on a list being tortured and experimented on. Then and now also shared my focus, which was solely on Samantha—to saving her—to being with her. *I can't let her die. I won't.*

I'd trusted the wrong people, that becoming crystal clear the moment Cal came for Sam. I thought I could remove us from the twisted game we'd all been playing since we were kids.

I'd been delusional.

I wouldn't make the same mistake twice. Sam was too useful for the powers that be to willingly hand her over to me. Fortunately, I still had an ace up my sleeve. Not a single living soul knew the full extent of my abilities and the fact that I could steal others' talents from them ... permanently.

But I had no idea what was going on outside of my prison, which made planning anything nearly impossible.

I will get out of here. And when I do there is going to be a reckoning.

Chapter 16
SAM

I sputtered and coughed as cold water was thrown into my face, the frigid temperature a slap to all my nerve endings. A bright light shone in my face, and I blinked away the white spots while trying to distinguish the faces that hovered around me.

"Tell her to connect with him mentally," an angry female voice demanded.

A large hand grabbed my chin, wrenching my head to the side. "You need to tell Austin what he's planning is pointless. We have you and therefore the power."

"What?" I didn't know what was going on. My mind reeled, grasping at what I'd just heard in order to figure it out. They didn't, whoever they were, give me a chance.

"Do it now." Fingers wound around my throat, squeezing.

"Okay," I croaked.

Sliding my eyes shut, I immediately found who I was

searching for. Despite my situation, connecting with Austin made warmth and comfort spread throughout my system. He made everything better, just like he always did.

"Sam, my Sammy girl." His deep voice was a familiar caress inside my mind, and just hearing it eased the pain in my heart … and my soul.

Without words, I conveyed as much as I could to him in a jumble of images. He deftly sorted through the mess, his anger rising within him. *"I'm coming for you. Just hang on. We have a plan."*

"We?" I murmured, unable to keep the word from slipping from my mouth. I peeked into his mind and saw—

"Nixon?" I gasped. "You're actually working with Nixon?"

Commotion erupted around me. "That's impossible!"

"What's going on?"

"Who's really with him?"

"Austin. Please. I need you. I need out of this place. I'm so confused. I don't—I don't know what's real anymore."

"We're real. Our love is real. Nothing else matters. If you lose sight of everything else, know that I love you. Trust in that truth." There was a pause before he spoke again, his voice hardening. *"You tell them that I'll give myself up. I'll stop fighting them. But only if we can be together. If they harm one hair on your head, I'll kill every last one of them."*

With that, he was abruptly gone from my mind, leaving me alone—completely alone. I whimpered at the sudden loss.

"What did he say?" The same fingers tightened around my neck. They must have been there the entire time, I'd just stopped noticing them.

"Let her go. She can't speak if you choke her." That's when I realized who the feminine voice belonged to.

Natalie.

"I should have known I couldn't trust you," I rasped. "Why? Why would you go through all of this trouble?"

"Austin is the only real currency I have with my ex-husband. And you, my dear, are the only way to control him."

"David's dead!" I screeched. "I saw him get shot!"

"Did you?" Natalie asked quietly. "Or did he just want you all to believe that you'd succeeded in killing him?"

I stilled. Was anything I thought to be true actually real? I choked back a sob. If David could manipulate us that much, then what else had we played into without the slightest clue?

"For what it's worth, I really do like you. I was hoping that your supposed death would flip Austin and you could live out the rest of your life with my son."

I blinked rapidly. "Your son?" She didn't have to answer for some of the missing pieces to click into place. "Nixon," I hissed.

"Yes. He's been obsessed with you for such a long time. I'm a bit concerned about how he's going to react if you end up dead."

I opened my mouth to respond, but laughter bubbled up and out of my chest instead. It was ridiculous. All of it.

"Now, tell me, what did Austin want you to relay to us?" Natalie demanded.

I swallowed my laughter, my lungs burning with the effort. "He said he'd come here—do what you want—" I sucked in a stuttering breath. "But he wants me—to be with me." I bit my cheek, my earlier hysterics merely morphing into demented giggles. "He's going to kill you all if you hurt me." My cheeks, my chest, my stomach, everything ached as fought to sober myself.

"Take her back to her cell. It looks like we'll be expecting company." They didn't have to question whether or not I was lying since I couldn't around Natalie.

A syringe was jabbed into my arm, the contents sweeping me under quickly.

I SENSED THEM WATCHING. I could feel their presence pressing in all around me. The small, rectangular viewing door had been left open. I was still a prisoner but was no longer cut off from other people's emotions. Only one person's mattered to me at the moment though—Austin. And yet I hadn't felt him in any way since he'd let me know he was coming for me. I didn't know what to think. But maybe the time for thinking was over. After all, I was an empath, and empaths lead with their emotions, not logic. I was going against nature. Perhaps now was the time to go with my instincts.

Uncurling from the floor, I slowly crept towards the

door, one agonizing step at a time. Unbidden, my mind flashed to an old memory. One better left buried.

I was eighteen years old, and somehow, even as an empath I'd managed to remain a virgin. I was on my way to my boyfriend's house, Donnie Sullivan. We'd been dating off and on for the last year, but over the past six months, things had been progressing steadily. My biggest issue was not knowing where his emotions ended and mine began when we were getting hot and heavy. A part of me wasn't sure if being around him at all was a good idea. We hadn't done much more than kiss and grope ... and yet, afterwards I always felt so ... dirty and alone. I had no one to talk to about it either.

Pushing down my inner conflict, I rang Donnie's doorbell. The red door swung open almost immediately, and Donnie pulled me into his house.

"My parents aren't home. They should be gone for another couple of hours." He tugged me after him, up the stairs and into his room, where he pushed me down on his bed, covering my body with his. "God, you're so fucking hot." His warm lips slanted over mine, his tongue plunging into my mouth. Only a moment of anxiety caused me to resist before his lust swept me under.

"I need you," I heard myself rasp. "Please, Donnie."

Somewhere in the back of my mind, I knew I wasn't ready to give my virginity to Donnie, but he was certainly ready to take it. My body was burning with need. Need that wasn't mine, not that I could physically tell the difference ... I just knew.

Things happened fast after that. The next thing I knew, Donnie had rolled on a condom and was pushing into me. I welcomed him into my body, knowing that I would regret it later. The rest was a blur. It was almost as if I partially blocked it out, not wanting to be a witness to my own folly.

Afterwards, when I was driving home, I had to pull my car over because I was sobbing so hard. I didn't and couldn't blame Donnie for what happened. He loved me. I could feel it. I didn't love him though. I'd never been given the chance to figure out what I really felt for him. I just wanted to be normal, something that I knew I could never be. Or at least in that moment I finally realized it. I hated myself—hated that something that should have been so wonderful was tearing me apart inside.

My thoughts snapped back to the present.

My first time should have been with Austin. My first and last and everything in between should have been with Austin. The parts of our childhood and teenage years together had been stolen from us. But on some level, I knew what I was missing. My love was reserved for Austin alone, and yet because I couldn't remember he existed, I gave my body to others like Donnie who didn't deserve it. Natalie and David, and the rest of them, had taken so much from us. All I wanted was Austin. All I'd ever want would be Austin, even when my mind couldn't remember him, my heart always did.

Rage seethed in me, burning, building. It gathered in my gut and coiled. I held it tight within me … waiting. I bit my tongue hard enough to draw blood, letting it dribble down my chin. "Help me!" I screamed, placing as much panic into my voice as I possibly could. "Please! Help me!" I shoved my face up to the opening in the door, showing the red froth I'd managed to produce for dramatic effect. "Please!"

A guard's face swung around to look at me, his expression scrunching up in a combination of disgust and uncertainty. "She's bleeding. What do we do?"

"Get a syringe and open the door. We can't let anything happen to her," the second guard snapped, obviously the one in charge.

As soon as the door opened, I let my rage fly. It was a tangible force that ripped into both of the guards, dropping them to the ground. This time my escape wasn't going to be a hallucination, dream, or anything else besides reality. It was time for a reckoning. I was done being played for the fool. I was done doing anything but winning the game. I was about to make my own rules.

Chapter 17

SAM

I'd been taught that anger was bad. Positive emotions held more power than their negative counterparts. Anger did nothing but damage. But what happens when damage is the ultimate goal? What happens if anger feels good … better than good because it equals finally being in control?

My life had been filled with lies heaped upon lies. Not using anger to empower myself seemed like just another falsehood to keep me under the thumbs of those who wished to control me. I would give myself over to all the darkness inside of me, all of the things I'd been fighting to suppress. I would finally give it free rein. The insidious taint within me was what made me different … stronger.

Austin and I shouldn't be in the positions we were in. No. We should be the ones dictating to everyone else because we were the ones with the most power. What we had inside of us trumped everything else. We just had to stop feeling guilty about using what we were born with.

I could no longer remember why it was such a bad idea. Maybe Chloe would have had something different to say, but she was gone. Dead and buried beneath all the pain she and Alex had endured. It was time for Samantha and Austin to do what they did best … survive.

I eyed the two guards on the floor who were writhing in pain. No alarms were going off, and no reinforcements had made their appearance yet. It all seemed too convenient. I'd fallen for that trick one too many times, unless it was my captors' arrogance that was going to allow me to escape. It was a possibility, however slim, but I wasn't going to bet on those low odds and let my guard down. I'd learned my lessons well. They'd been beaten into me repeatedly over the years.

I pulled a small handgun from a hip holster on the guard closest to me and then removed the holster itself. After I'd adorned my own body with my new weapon, I ripped the set of keys off of guard number two.

My gaze roamed over the doors that lined the fluorescent-lit hallway. A flash of my faux escape from before played across my mind, and I decided that even though I still had no idea if I'd escaped and been recaptured, or if it had all been an illusion, I wasn't going to repeat my prior actions of unlocking any doors.

The eerie silence, as I made my way warily down the corridor, set my nerves on edge. It was too quiet. Someone had to know I'd been let out of my cage. Which only pointed to the fact that I was being released, but for what purpose? There was always some ulterior motive that I wasn't privy to when Natalie and David were involved. Was I being used to lure Austin in again, or to destroy him completely? It was no secret that the first thing I would do upon escaping would be to find him.

"Fuck," I swore under my breath.

My only hope was to do the exact opposite of what was expected of me, which would mean not immediately tracking down Austin. But then what would happen if he came for me like he planned, and I wasn't here?

Confusion washed over me, replacing my anger, my driving force. I didn't have a plan or a place to go. All I knew was that I had to get away from what I'd come to think of as my own personal hell.

And yet … yet … I was frozen with uncertainty. *What the hell is wrong with you? Run!* My own voice screamed in my head. It seemed so far away though.

Spinning in a circle, I tried to determine the best direction to go. *Austin!* I mentally called out. *Why can't I feel you? Austin!*

"I'm right here Sam, my beautiful Sammy girl."

No. I don't believe it. I can't let myself believe it. It's another trick—an illusion—an auditory hallucination. But then his mind opened to me, and I fell headlong into him, just as his large hands turned me towards him.

Blinking back tears, I stared up into his impossibly bright azure eyes as his callused fingertips danced over the contours of my face. Our emotions hummed around each other's, mingling … sharing everything. We remained like that for an eternity before a strangled cry burst from my lungs, and I threw myself into his arms, wrapping my legs around his waist. I slammed my lips into his, not caring if I hurt either of us. This kind of pain would be welcome.

Austin pressed me into the wall savagely, and I rocked up into him, desperation riding me hard. I needed him more than I needed my next breath. I would die happy as long as I got one last time with him. Nothing else mattered.

"No," Austin rumbled, breaking away from me. "I want more than one last time with you." I tried to follow his lips with mine as he forced me to disentangle myself from him. "We need to leave now."

I nodded in agreement even though my body screamed out for more of his touch. I wanted nothing more than to feel him moving inside of me, consequences be damned.

Austin snagged my gaze with a heated one, making my thighs clench together. "Soon." He took my hand within his, leading me down the hallway.

"Where is everyone? How did you get in here? What about everyone else they have locked away here?"

"I'll explain everything later. There's no time now."

"Where's Nixon?"

Austin didn't respond, his mind closing off to me. I bit my lip, knowing that none of my questions would be answered at the moment. I trusted Austin though—of course—and I had him back. The rest could wait.

We didn't pass one single person on the way out of the building. More and more questions were compiling in my head. I couldn't help it. How many times had things seemed to be too convenient only to later find out that they were indeed? "Austin, you have to give me something. I need to know what the hell is going on."

"I can't answer that now," he responded tersely while moving quickly to an idling black SUV.

Frustration welled up in me. Again, I pushed it down. He had to have a good reason for acting the way he was. After all, we were escaping, or he was rescuing me. It was probably not the best time to stop for a debriefing of any kind. It was just after going for so long without any answers ... I needed them.

Inside of the SUV, sitting in the driver's seat was Nixon. His dark gaze flicked to me briefly, but he remained silent until Austin spoke to him. "Did you get the files?"

Nixon nodded. "Yep."

"Then let's get the hell out of here." Austin slid into the back seat with me, pulling me into his side.

I rested my head on his chest and wrapped my arms around his waist. I was exhausted, and as I inhaled his spicy aroma, the mental and physical abuse all caught up with me. Feeling completely safe for the first time in a long time, I didn't fight as my eyes fluttered shut.

Chapter 18
NIXON

My cell door swung open to reveal Natalie. I stopped thinking of her as my mother years ago. I only used the moniker when it suited me, as in when I thought that I could possibly sway her to do something for me. Like now.

"Mother."

She tilted her head, studying me for a moment before responding, "Samantha has escaped."

I ground my teeth together. Her little visit made sense. She needed me to do something for her … again. We liked to use each other. I hated the thought that we might be more alike than I'd ever admit. "How is that my problem? Apparently, I don't rate better than the other inmates here."

"Don't be so dramatic, Nixon. I had to put you in here for your own good. Your obsession, yours and Austin's both, is unhealthy. I don't think—"

"Austin," I hissed. I instinctively knew exactly how Sam had gotten out. "He came for her, didn't he? And you let him just waltz out of here with her in tow?" A humorless laugh escaped me. "With all your people and all your equipment—with all your carefully constructed plans and side dealings—you didn't see that coming?"

"There's an individual with Austin who is pretending to be you. Cal is dead and the other Nixon is a completely unknown quantity. No one saw him coming."

The vision of Sam dying in my arms replayed in my mind's eye. If that was the truth, then Sam might not die in my arms at all; this imposter Nixon could be out to proactively kill her. It wouldn't be the first time someone was gunning for her. Even though I wanted to tell Natalie to fuck off, I couldn't after the information she just shared with me. I'd do what she needed me to do until the opportunity to take Sam and run again presented itself.

"I can read you like a book, Nixon. It's written all over your face. You still want to disappear with her." She leaned up against the doorframe, and I pulled myself up to my full height. "I'll make you a deal. You kill Austin, and you can have her. I won't interfere anymore if you can do that for me."

My jaw dropped. "After all this time ... he's been the main objective and suddenly you want him dead? I don't understand." I scrubbed a hand over my face in confusion. Not that I exactly had a problem with killing Austin. After all, I'd been planning on doing it anyways.

"We've finally realized he can't be controlled."

"You're just now realizing this?" *I should just kill her and take her ability. I should kill them all ... all except Sam.* No matter what Natalie said, it was probably the only real way any of us would truly be left alone.

Natalie turned, leaving her back to me. She obviously couldn't begin to fathom that I might actually despise her. Bad mothers seemed to be without a clue that they were actually ... bad mothers. "Use whatever resources you need and any means possible."

The door was left wide open, but I was frozen in place. Her heels clicked their way down the hallway and disappeared. I was unnerved. After years of playing all of us like pieces on a chess board, and suddenly the entire game had changed? Or they just wanted me to think it had? Nothing was ever the way it seemed. I'd learned that at a very young age. But I wasn't going to look too closely at my newfound freedom and mission. As soon as Austin was dead, and I had his abilities ... Sam and their unshakable bond would be mine.

Chapter 19
SAM

"Sammy," Austin murmured, his full, soft lips skimming across the bare skin on my shoulder.

I groaned, rolling towards his voice. I was afraid to open my eyes in case I was dreaming.

"You're not, dreaming that is." His lips slid up my neck and pressed firmly against mine.

I tunneled my fingers into his hair, pulling him tightly against me. His scent, his taste ... the feel of his hard body against mine—pure bliss. A bliss I never thought I'd get to feel again. I'd hoped, but deep down, there was a part of me that was terrified to admit how much I'd been terrified of never seeing the man I loved outside of my mind again.

"I need you," I breathed into his mouth.

Since I was apparently already naked, Austin found his way into me quickly. I wrapped my legs around his waist, resting my feet just above his perfectly defined ass. Only then did I allow myself to slit my eyes open. Through the thick fringe of my lashes, I watched as Austin's face took in my reactions to his pistoning hips. He studied me intently, his gaze locked on me. Just like always, our thoughts intertwined so our minds and bodies could be one. And yet I was still very much aware that all of my lust and raw emotions stemmed from inside of me.

Austin always knew just where to touch for exactly the right amount of time. He owned every part of me, just like I owned every molecule inside of him. I scored my nails down his back, crying out his name as I fell over the cliff, my orgasm ripping through my system, tearing me to pieces, only to be heightened when I felt Austin's own release pulsing into me. It was over much too quickly, but I also knew there'd be more. Because I'd always want more when it came to my Austin.

MY QUESTIONS HAD TEMPORARILY BEEN FORGOTTEN, PUSHED by the wayside by the need to get carnally reacquainted with Austin. Even in the afterglow, my mind had been blissfully peaceful, and very uncomplicated. But now that we were both, for the time being, satiated, all of my prior worries had come rushing back to me.

"We need to talk," I croaked, wishing like hell we didn't. Not that I didn't enjoy talking to my husband, but I wished what I had on my mind could be mundane subject matter. Definitely not conspiracies, death addictions, and basically … the reality that had become our lives.

"I know," Austin rasped, his warm breath fanning the top of my head. He curled his arm tightly around my waist, pulling me more firmly into his side. His callused fingers kneaded my soft flesh gently.

I stretched, licked my lips, and resisted the urge to bite his nipple, knowing it would probably instigate another round of—

Wait. Why didn't I want to do that again? My heart sped up and I rubbed my thighs together. A little bit longer of a reprieve wouldn't be such a bad idea … especially if it meant more sex with the man I loved. I could never get enough of him.

"Sam," Austin growled playfully. "I'm completely on board with where your thoughts are going, but you're right, we need to talk."

"I'll just take a peek in your brain … much faster," I murmured. "And then we can get back to business."

The only problem was that when I tried to push further into Austin's mind, there was a block—or rather, he was hiding something from me in the dark recesses of his consciousness. It only made me want—no, *need* to know what he was keeping from me. We didn't keep secrets from each other, at least not anymore.

"No," he grated. "Don't."

Ignoring his warning, I bulldozed right past his blocks before he could strengthen them.

"The list." Nixon gave Austin a furtive glance from the driver's seat of the SUV. When Austin didn't respond, Nixon pressed more. "You remember the list that Sam and I found with

all the names?" Austin still ignored him. "All of our real names?"

"Yeah?" Austin snapped with irritation. "You going somewhere with this?"

"Actually yes, I am."

"Spit it out then."

"We already know that everyone on that list is, or in some cases was, like us, and they all were experimented on."

"Yeah, so?"

"You, Sam, Malcolm, and Maggie weren't the first to be honed for being the perfect assassins." Austin was staring blankly out the window as if he couldn't care less. "This is important, man," Nixon ground out.

Austin turned his lackluster gaze to Nixon. "I'm still waiting for you to make a point."

Nixon began to drone on, or at least that's how it seemed to Austin, but then a phrase, or a number really, caught his attention. The number fifteen. Something I didn't understand happened next. A kind of haze dropped down over Austin, and his mind conjured an image of Jake. Which I was sure Austin had gleaned from his connection to me at some point. But it was more than that. At the mere mention of the number fifteen combined with a series of other random words, Austin was suddenly fixated on thoughts of Jake ... and killing him.

A series of events passed in a blur, as if I was fast-forwarding through them, culminating with the arrival of Austin at the building I had been kept in. Abruptly, the scene crystallized, and Austin stared down at Jake as he eagerly wrapped his fingers around his neck.

Austin was unclear on his rationale for his violence, but in the end, he didn't care, the death would be one he could and would enjoy. For a brief moment, Austin's mind sought mine out, but something in him prevented our connection from being opened. Ultimately, he gave himself completely over to the experience as he drank down Jake's death emotions—fear, regret, anguish, and finally acceptance. He reveled in his first cold-blooded kill of a completely innocent soul, and he did it all on his own. When Jake's last breath slipped from his lungs, and Austin inhaled with joy—only then did the slightest bit of guilt worm its way into his system.

The very next thing he was aware of … he was coming for me. The rest I already knew because I had experienced it right alongside him.

"Austin!" I gasped. My fingers dug into his chest as I levered myself up to straddle him. "What was that? I don't understand … what happened?"

His chest rose and fell rapidly, and his eyes had darkened with a kind of wildness that I was unfamiliar with. "I-I don't know." Austin pushed me off of him and sat up, his legs dangling over the side of the bed, and his elbows rested on his knees. "I have no real explanation for why I killed him, but I liked it. I fucking liked it. Please tell me you understand."

I slid my hands up the wide expanse of his back, pressing myself into him. "I do, but I still don't understand what happened. I don't understand any of what's been happening. As time goes on and the more information we get—the less I understand."

I was trying to remain calm, or at least attempting to convince myself that I actually was calm. Whatever had been done to Austin, had to do with me, and my dream about the number fifteen. Our lives had taken on a dreamlike or surreal state. Our sanity was questionable. I was missing huge pieces of the puzzle, probably even my memory still. I was sure Austin was just as confused, if not more so than me.

Tightening my grip, I pressed into him. "We're together again. That's all that matters. We'll figure the rest out." I pressed a kiss to his shoulder. "I love you. Nothing will ever change that."

And in truth, that was the scariest thought of all. Austin could become just like Malcolm, and I would never turn away from him. Never.

Chapter 20

SAM

I stared at Austin as he slept. His face in repose was that of an angel. *And he is my angel. He's everything good in my life.* Without him … well, without him, I didn't know where I'd be, and it didn't really matter. 'What-ifs' in life were pointless. No one could go back and change anything, so worrying about all the things they could have done differently was a waste of time. All anyone could do was push forward and look to the future.

I ran a hand through Austin's dark sex and sleep-mussed hair. He made a happy little grunting noise and nuzzled my stomach. I bit my cheek to keep from laughing. I wished with all my being that things could always be so simple for Austin and me, but I knew they couldn't.

The truth is … I'm terrified.

Our minds had been tampered with. And until you've

had someone kicking around in your head, that level of fear can never quite be explained. One's mind should always be off limits to anyone but yourself unless permission is given for it to be otherwise. How could Austin and I protect each other when we didn't even know if we could? What if I was some kind of assassin already, and I wasn't aware of it? What if he was? I wasn't oblivious to the brainwashing trope in fiction and all of the outlandish intricacies it involved. Only now it didn't seem quite so ridiculous. What happened with Austin and Jake—that was some serious programming shit that you might see in a spy movie or tv series.

"Sam," Austin's breath tickled and warmed my bare stomach simultaneously, "I can feel your anxiety."

I nibbled my lower lip. "I'm scared, Austin."

"Don't be. We'll figure it out. We'll end up on top. You'll see."

I slipped out from under him, his head flopping down to the mattress. "That's the thing though—when have we ever ended up on top?" His baby blues studied me intensely. "We haven't. Ever since we were kids in that hospital, it's been one thing after another, we just didn't remember any of it. I didn't remember you."

I pulled my knees up to my chest and wrapped my arms around my legs. "You've been stolen from me so many times." I fought to swallow back the bile in my throat. "What if they do it again?"

Austin rose from his reclining position, and as he scooted across the bed towards me, I couldn't help but take in the long, lean muscles that flexed and rippled across his chest and abs. I suddenly wanted to forget everything but him ... again.

"They could never permanently separate us, and they never will."

I licked my lips. "Never say never."

"Sammy ... my beautiful, good Sammy girl. You and me, we're eternal. Since that first time you walked into my hospital room when we were kids ... It was you and me against the world. I love you." He wrapped his arms around me, and I went limp against him as I closed my eyes.

"I love you so much, Austin, and that's what scares me. They've done things to us. How do we even know that we're not playing into their hands right now?"

I could tell by the way that his muscles tensed that Austin knew what I'd just said was worth consideration because it could be true. "We're going to leave the country. We'll disappear."

"What's in those files that Nixon stole?" The curiosity was finally too much for me to ignore.

Austin's exhaled loudly. "It's a list of everyone that was in that hospital with us. It—"

"But we already had that list—"

Austin shook his head, stirring my hair. "No, this list has all the names, and where they are now. Also, what their abilities are. It has everything when the old list was incomplete."

"We're in the files, too?"

"I'm assuming yes."

A feeling of unease pushed at me. Something wasn't right. "Why did Nixon want those files?"

"I didn't stop to give him the third degree. I just wanted you out of that place."

I pulled away from Austin, looking deep into his eyes. "We need to get a look at those files."

"Nixon's gone."

"What do you mean he's gone?" My voice shot up an octave. "Does that seem right to you? Something—" I jumped up and started pacing. "No, we need to find him and those files. It's important."

"Sam, calm down. We—"

"This is a mistake, Austin. We're not going to run away, and we're done being complacent. With that information, maybe once and for all we can put an end to all of this. For all we know, what's been done to us is in those files—our very salvation could be in those files. H-How could you not have thought about all of that?"

"I-I don't know. I guess I was so focused on all of the rest—on you." Austin rolled out of bed and began yanking on his clothes.

A small part of me was sad to see him get dressed, but with a little luck maybe one day we could just be a normal married couple with a normal … okay, normal-ish married couple with a normal-ish life, and I could enjoy my husband at my leisure without life-altering matters hanging in the balance. "Nixon can't be that far off. We'll find him and we'll get those files."

I still couldn't shake the mild panic that had settled around us, but I knew going after that information was a step in the right direction. I could just *feel* it.

Chapter 21

SAM

Austin and I drove in complete silence. The tension that hung between us wasn't the kind that threatened the solidarity of our relationship, or even the kind that could cause a fight. It merely kept me from speaking what was on my mind. It was as if the chunk of time since Austin had let Taryn die and Cal had stolen him away from me felt like a dream. My life had taken on a surreal quality, and it wasn't the first time I'd lamented that fact.

But suddenly the fog had lifted, and I was focused, my eyes wide open. I'd done a ton of stupid shit that I couldn't quite figure out how I'd let myself rationalize my decisions away. Things seemed somehow simpler now. We would find the files, we would get the information we needed to free ourselves, and then we'd live out our lives the way we wanted. As long as Austin and I were together, we could and would make that happen.

And yet, I knew Austin was craving the feel of death emotions. His mind was locked onto it, and despite his attempts to conceal it from me, he couldn't. Oddly, I took it as a good sign that he was trying to hide it at all. As long as he still had a small amount of shame left then it wasn't too late, my Austin—or maybe I should say my Alex—wasn't lost to me.

"Austin," I murmured, sliding my hand over to the center console of the SUV to touch his elbow. "Don't hide it from me, maybe I can help."

He shook his head slowly while keeping his eyes on the road. "I want it. I can't stop thinking about it. It's almost as if a little voice inside of my head is screaming at me that there's nothing wrong with it. It keeps telling me that I should just give in now—that we should just give in." He swallowed audibly. "Do you think about what it would be like for us to be like we were after the blast, but whenever we wanted?"

"All the time," I whispered.

The SUV lurched to the side of the road, skidding to an abrupt stop. Austin grabbed me, taking my face between his hands. "Then why don't we? What's stopping us?" His gaze hungrily searched mine, pleading for permission.

My heart dropped into my stomach even as my blood heated. *All I have to do is say yes. Wouldn't be simpler if I did?* I slid my gaze away from his. "We can't. We just can't."

He pulled away from me, hitting the steering wheel

with his fist. "Why the fuck not? What's actually stopping us?"

"I … don't—" I slumped against the window, sighing heavily. "My conscience. I still have one."

Austin nodded his head rapidly. "Okay, yeah, so we just kill murderers, rapists, scum like that. We could do the kind of work we were doing, but not with Natalie. We could—"

"And what happens when it's not enough? What happens when their deaths aren't satisfying anymore?"

Austin gripped the steering wheel as his jaw muscles feathered. "It will just have to be enough."

I opened and shut my mouth several times, not sure how to respond. I wanted to agree with him—after all, it would be simpler—but I knew in my gut that it wouldn't be enough. Just like any other addiction, it would eventually escalate. Instead of voicing what I knew Austin had to be picking up from me already, I said the only other thing I could in that moment. "I love you."

He turned back towards me, his azure gaze filled with anguish. "And I think that's the only thing that's stopping me, Sam. You—your love." He abruptly leaned forward, pulling me into his arms, his face pushing into my hair. "Don't stop. Please don't ever stop. Because I don't think I'd even know who I am anymore if it wasn't for you."

He was cracking, and it shattered my heart. "We need to find Nixon and those files." Just like I always did, I decided to grab onto something to keep us moving forward, something in the future to focus on. We had a plan after all, and I had no choice but to believe that we would get out of this alive.

Austin nodded slowly as he turned back towards the steering wheel. After another long exhale he threw the SUV into drive and pulled back onto the highway. Silence engulfed us once more.

Chapter 22
AUSTIN

My attempt to hide it from her was weak at best, although I'm not sure why I bothered at all.

The craving for it consumed me.

Death ... death ... death ...

It spun around and around in my head, ricocheting endlessly in my skull, driving me to the brink of insanity. I knew I would need to feed the addiction to find any semblance of respite. Killing Jake had taken the edge off, but it wasn't enough, not nearly enough. At least I temporarily didn't have to worry about Nixon and his own addiction, which was my wife.

I glanced at Sam, who was curled up in the center of our hotel bed, burrowed beneath the covers. She'd passed out almost as soon as her head hit the pillow.

She's exhausted, so she'll be asleep for a while. She wouldn't have to know.

My gaze darted back to Sam, afraid that she'd heard my thoughts even while unconscious, the guilt of them eating at me. And yet the small voice in the back of my head was getting louder.

You could sneak out and be back before she wakes up.

I stared at her another few moments, waging an internal battle before I slipped from the bed and hastily threw my clothes on.

Next time—next time we can do it together.

Now that thought actually brought a smile to my face and anticipation to my gut.

Chapter 23

SAM

Austin stalked his prey with nervous anticipation. The short, balding man was a murderer and a thief. The prior crime obviously worse than the latter. He'd beaten his stepson to death after one of his nightly alcohol binges. It hadn't stopped him from imbibing though. In fact, he was currently so shit-faced, he couldn't even walk straight. Austin felt justified in his choice of victim. He would enjoy the man's death twice as much because of it.

When Austin followed him into his dark house and slipped his hands around the man's neck, I found myself egging him on mentally. Austin's heart beat hard, adrenaline pumping through his system. The man's thought process was slower than normal because of his intoxication level, but—

I arched up, breathing in tandem with Austin. It didn't matter. The regret and surprise of this man's death was still sweet. We drank it down together, me, an unwilling and yet thankful passenger in my husband's mind.

"Sammy, I love you," Austin muttered under his breath as the man's limp body fell from his hands.

I numbly noted that Austin seemed to prefer to choke his victims. At least he'd choked his latest, and Jake as well. I wondered what it meant. Not that I cared all that much in the moment.

"Austin, please come back to me. I need you."

How could I have tried to resist this?

Austin was right. Why should we stop? What was wrong with it really? The man whose death we'd just enjoyed wouldn't be missed. He was a blight on society. As long as we took out people like him, why shouldn't we enjoy ourselves in the process? I couldn't remember the reasons why I'd thought it was a bad idea before.

By the time Austin made it back to the hotel, I was half out of my mind with lust. As soon as he opened the door to our room, I launched myself at him.

Austin and I had always had beautiful chemistry together and beyond amazing sex. Add in the desperation of almost having lost each other so many times, compile that with the heightened emotions brought on by feeling someone else's death, and … nothing, no words could describe how much I needed to feel every inch of Austin touching every inch of my body.

We didn't make it to the bed, or even close to it. We were lucky he'd managed to shut the door. His mouth consumed mine while I devoured his flesh with hungry hands. Austin sliding into my writhing body was more than sex, it was me welcoming the other half of my soul back inside of me.

Gibberish danced off my tongue, my body and mind trying to make sense of what was happening to it, the sensations too much and simultaneously not enough.

My entire world had narrowed down to Austin.

His fingers bit into my hips as he pounded into me, harder, harder, harder … It wasn't enough. It would never be enough. I needed more. I would always need more.

I screamed his name as a kaleidoscope of colors exploded behind my eyes. Too much. It was too much. I was too sensitive. Too. Much. And yet …

It still wasn't enough. I needed more … more … more …

Austin, please.

"I'm right there with you, baby. I'm right there—fuuuuck!" Austin jerked his hips against me roughly as he pulsed his release.

I continued to rock against him, ignoring the hiss he made. I didn't care. I wasn't done yet. I'd never be done.

Only a few heartbeats passed before Austin surged back to life inside of me. He leaned down, grabbing my legs behind my knees, and pushed them up onto his shoulders. "I'll never be done with you either." He delivered me a cocky and yet dazzling grin before he began to move again.

His hands slid up to pinch my nipples. I moaned loudly.

"I'm going to make sure you can't walk tomorrow." The grin on his face grew, and despite the reason of how we'd gotten there, I was loving the return of the old, over-confident, and egotistical Austin.

"Shut up and fuck me," I demanded.

And he of course obliged.

AUSTIN and I often tried to fix our relationship problems with sex. Deep down, we both knew that nothing was resolved by that particular method, but we certainly felt a hell of a lot better afterwards. Sex went beyond the physical for Austin and me. It was about feeling connected and expressing our love. It gave us a chance to ignore the rest of the world as it temporarily fell away. No task seemed too complicated or large to tackle after we'd thoroughly loved each other in such a way.

A loud knock thudded against our hotel room, and I sucked in a startled breath, sitting up from my lounging position across Austin's chest. He tensed beneath me. Our gazes locked for a millisecond before we were both on our feet and scrambling for our clothes. When we were both haphazardly dressed, Austin crept to the door, checking the peephole. He then hesitantly undid the locks and—

A body toppled into the room.

I choked back a scream, the bulk of it lodging in my chest. Frozen, I stared at the lifeless hotel maid. Her long, dark hair had come loose from a French braid, the ends tipped in crimson. Her throat had been slit, and blood had seeped into her uniform, already dried. The gash in her neck was deep enough that if her head lolled to the side, I was positive I'd see bone. I couldn't tell just by looking at her how long she'd been dead, but obviously long enough for the blood to dry since it was only on her and not the carpet or door.

"What the fuck?" I muttered.

Austin's nostrils flared with agitation. "Someone is trying to make a point."

He slid his arms under the body, dragging it fully into our room, and dropped it haphazardly at his feet. He then kicked the door shut behind him. Normally he would have been careful to not touch the body without gloves or some kind of barrier, but it was obvious to the both of us that precautions would be worthless in this instance. Someone was trying to make a point, although I wasn't exactly sure what it was just yet.

"No one's seen her yet or the cops would already be at our door," Austin mumbled more to himself than me.

"This could be a setup and they could be on their way. I'll get our stuff." Adrenaline pumping through my system, I raced around gathering what little things we had. When I'd finished, Austin was still crouched over her body. I stopped short when he slipped in to feel her death emotions, pulling me along for the ride.

I can't believe Susan called off work again today. I was planning on sleeping in, vegging out, and yep, that's about it. Classes start back up in a week, and then I'll get absolutely no downtime. Days off will be spent studying or in class. I suppose a little bit of extra cash couldn't hurt. I really need to get a better job, but until I have my degree, I'm kind of limited. Manny always makes sure my work schedule doesn't interfere with my classes.

Heaving a huge sigh, I slide the key card in the slot and the light blips green. I push the cart up to the wall, grab my cleaning supplies, and amble slowly into the room. I really wish I was still sleeping. I hum to myself as I work. Just a few more hours and I can go back to sleep. My bed is literally calling my name.

The sound of the door clicking shut startles me, and I look up just in time to see a man step into the bathroom behind me. Our gazes meet for a brief moment. He's handsome and yet there is something dark in his eyes. Fear courses through my system. I open my mouth to scream, but he's already on me, his hand pressing into my mouth. I try to bite the fleshy part of his palm, but the glint of something shiny catches my attention in the mirror. I watch in horror as my throat is slit.

This can't be happening. I should have tried to fight him. I didn't do anything.

The man steps away from me ... and smiles. His gaze remains on me as I clutch at my throat, trying to keep the blood in as I collapse to the floor. Warmth surrounds me, and yet I'm so cold. I sputter and choke on my own blood. Spots dance before my eyes, and I can't help but curse Susan out in my head for calling off work today. I should be at home in bed. I should—

Austin pivoted to face me with wild eyes. The man in the mirror, the murderer, was Nixon. And because of what we just witnessed, neither one of us could fully enjoy the death. I guiltily pushed down those regrets.

"I thought you could only feel the death emotions of people as they were dying. I thought only I could feel the death emotions of people after they were dead."

Austin, of course, had enjoyed both with me, but it was the first time I was aware that he'd slipped in without using my help at all. I knew that I used some of his abilities, so was it possible he was using mine now?

He nodded as he picked my thoughts out of my head. "Yeah, our abilities are more mingled than before."

I filed that away for later. There were quite a few things that Austin could do that I couldn't, at least before I couldn't, maybe now was different. "There has to be some kind of mistake. Why would Nixon kill her and leave her on our doorstep?"

"Something's not right."

I snorted. "Something is always not right."

"Let's get going. Finding him is even more imperative now."

I trailed along behind Austin, not sparing the dead girl another glance. My focus now was on tracking down Nixon. It really was a statement of how far we'd fallen. We used to care about things like dead girls and justice. Now, all I really cared about was Austin. He'd once offhandedly remarked that all real love was based a bit on obsession, and I could confirm that as truth. Even Malcolm, with his numerous faults, had loved Maggie. *We're just like them now.*

"No. No, we're not. We'll never be like them," Austin growled. He took my hand in his, squeezing tightly as he tugged me along after him.

I realized I didn't even know where we were, state-wise. I'd been so disoriented and then fully distracted by getting reacquainted with my husband. "Where are we?"

"West Virginia," Austin grunted.

"Is that where I was being held?"

"Yes."

"It fucking figures. If there is a hell on earth, damn straight it's in West Virginia."

Austin opened the SUV's doors with the automatic lock, and I flung my bag into the back seat before sliding into the passenger seat. "Where are we headed?"

He jammed the key in the ignition and started the engine. "Don't know. But we need to put some space between us and here."

"Pittsburgh," I muttered, running my hands through my hair. "We need to go to Pittsburgh."

Austin turned towards me, lifting a quizzical eyebrow. "Why Pittsburgh exactly?"

I lifted my arms and let them drop with defeat. "Because that's where this shit always ends up. Just a gut instinct."

Shrugging, Austin threw the SUV into drive and pulled out of the parking lot. "Pittsburgh it is then."

Chapter 24
NIXON

Rage simmered in my gut as I stared down at the body on the floor of the hotel room. Austin was killing with Sam. *My Sam.* I didn't care what anyone said. Sam had feelings for me after all the years we'd spent together as a married couple. She could deny it all she wanted, but I saw the truth in my visions with our potential shared future. She could and would be happy with me. It didn't matter if our relationship was built on lies. After all, weren't most relationships?

And now Austin was doing exactly what I always knew he'd do … He was dragging her down with him. Even though I planned on stealing his abilities—to do whatever she needed to thrive, even if that meant killing. I would always do my best to pull her out of it. Austin reveled in the darkness. Austin was selfish. Austin was—

"I'm going to kill him with my bare hands," I growled.

I'd wanted to kill Austin for a long time. The fact that my mother now sanctioned his death almost had me wanting to keep him alive out of spite for her, but after this …

Dead, dead, dead. He's already dead, he just doesn't fucking know it yet.

Girls like Sam were drawn to the bad boy. They wanted things they shouldn't. Austin was a cliché—a fucking joke. The problem was, the more that people tried to separate her from him, the tighter she clung to him. I would just have to find someone to wipe her memory again. Or, after I killed Austin and had possession of his abilities, I could do it myself. I'd see to it one way or another that Sam never remembered Austin. It would be like he never existed at all.

All I had to do was track them down. Which would be pretty easy, since I'd merely have to follow the trail of dead bodies.

Chapter 25
SAM

My last trip to Pittsburgh had been with Nixon to follow a lead. We'd subsequently stumbled upon two empaths who knew each other and who both ended up dead minutes within us meeting them. One of the empaths had also been harboring a list that contained the birth names of all of the people who'd been at the hospital with us as children.

I sighed heavily as I stared out the window. Pittsburgh. Why did everything keep leading back to Pittsburgh? It was my hometown, and it would always be a part of me, but I didn't like getting dragged back for one reason or another. Especially since my trips always ended in blood and death lately. So far, I'd personally gotten out relatively unscathed, but if I kept testing the limits of my birth city's grace, I wasn't sure my luck would hold.

I glanced over at Austin as he drove. His features were

pinched with intense focus, his thoughts clearly elsewhere. "I guess we should get a hotel?"

"Yeah," Austin responded after a moment.

I pushed at Austin's mind, wanting and yet afraid to know what I'd find. A block went up immediately. I huffed in annoyance. "I hate when you do that."

The corner of Austin's full lips tipped up. "I thought you didn't like it when I prodded around in your mind. You don't get free rein in mine if that's the case."

"Fine, whatever."

It didn't bother me so much anymore, at least not like it used to. After everything we'd been through, even his more annoying personality traits were welcome just as long as he was close to me. He rarely gave me any personal space physically or mentally. And he was controlling and possessive. Also, he was controlling, jealous, and—

"I love you, Austin." The words tumbled from my mouth as my heart clenched. Despite his flaws, I loved him, all of him, the good and the bad, desperately and unendingly.

A sudden wave of anxiety crashed over me. "We should just run away. Live in Hawaii or the Bahamas—Bora Bora."

After smoothly rolling the SUV to the side of the road, Austin tugged me towards him, his rough palm abrading my cheek. "You were right. We need to figure this all out, or we'll never be free. If we just run, we'll be looking over our shoulders for the rest of our lives. And maybe our children's lives."

My heart took off at a gallop. I did want children someday. It was just a topic that I'd never permitted myself to consider seriously. The image of Austin when I'd first met him sprang up in my mind unbidden. Would our son have the same dark hair and blue eyes as him? My insides squeezed at the thought. "I want ... I want a family with you."

Was it even possible? How could we raise a child or children with our death addictions? We weren't fit to be parents no matter how much I wanted that to be a lie. My face scrunched up against my will as I tried to stave off tears. "We can't, Austin. We can never have that."

Austin scowled as he met my gaze, his baby blues ensnaring me in their fathomless depths. "We deserve to be happy, and goddamnit, Sam, it's going to happen. We're going to be happy."

Silence thickened the air between us as he settled back into his seat and threw the SUV back into drive. "We'll stay at the Sheraton in Station Square." Austin's voice was devoid of all emotion, which usually meant he was feeling too much at the moment.

"Austin ..." I swallowed the rest of my words, knowing nothing I could say would comfort him—us. I agreed that we deserved more, a chance at a normal life, but we hadn't been dealt those cards. We had to do the best we could with what we had been given, and at least that included each other. *As long as we have each other, nothing can be that bad.*

AUSTIN and I had fallen into bed together as soon as we were in our new hotel room. We were both seeking comfort from each other. It was as if with each touch, each stroke, and each kiss, we were assuring ourselves that we could possibly have the life we dreamt of.

It was all a lie, and we both knew it.

"My beautiful, good Sammy girl," Austin rasped, his lips skimming over my neck. "I wish—" He raised his head so he could meet my gaze. His azure eyes seemed darker with the weight of everything that was swimming in them. "I just wish—"

"Shhh." I let my fingers dance along his sculpted features, scaling my nails softly over the scuff on his face. "I know."

We kept going in circles, the two of us. We'd bonded as children, only to be ripped from each other's lives, our memories erased. Then when we were older, after our sordid love affair, me cheating on Nixon, and him on Jessica, we'd managed to find happiness with each other ... only to be ripped apart and my memories tampered with. Time and time again we were torn apart, and yet somehow, we always found our way back to each other. Eventually, the cycle would be broken, for better or worse.

Things simply couldn't keep going on the way they had been indefinitely.

I pulled Austin down to me, and he wrapped his arms under me, resting his head on my chest. His warm breath tickled, causing goose bumps to race across my skin in quick succession. I threaded my hands in his hair and leaned back against the headboard, letting my eyes slide shut. My breathing slowed to match his, and I felt his eyelashes flutter shut.

In that moment, despite what the future might bring, I was content … happy even. Austin loved me in a way that no other man ever could. Some women never got to experience that kind of unconditional love in their lives. Even if Austin and I died, at least I'd gotten to feel it—to have him for a short period of time. At least I'd had him at all.

I walked through the department store, letting my eyes slide over the brightly colored fabrics. I wasn't sure what I was looking for, but I had a feeling I'd know when I found it.

A long, red dress, hanging on one of the mannequins caught my attention. The top part was see-through lace, with material covering all the right places, and the skirt would hug me faultlessly. It was sexy, and yet not overtly so. It was daring and not risqué. It was perfect. I scanned the area around the display so I could find the dress in my size—

"Oh my God!" someone screamed, followed by a rapid pop-pop-pop sound.

High-pitched screams filled the air. People ran past me with terror etched into their faces. I turned slowly, and yet somehow I already knew what I'd find. There was a man holding a small handgun with a silencer standing no more than a dozen feet away from me. I glanced at the bodies he'd left in his wake. Some were dead, and some were dying. He raised the gun higher and took aim. Just before he pulled the trigger, he took a step closer to me and uttered one word harshly.

"Fifteen."

And then he pulled the trigger.

I sat up in bed, gasping for air, an all too familiar sensation of dread surrounding me. How many times over the years had I been startled awake after a disturbing dream or vision? Too many to count, that was for sure.

"Austin?" I called out when I realized that he was no longer holding me or anywhere to be seen. There was no light in the bathroom either. I stumbled from the bed, searching the hotel room. He was nowhere to be found.

"Shit." My stomach twisted into a knot. I already knew where he was. He hadn't been able to resist the pull of another kill.

I sank to my knees right in the middle of the floor and dropped my face into my hands.

It was too late. After everything we'd been through, it was already too late.

Chapter 26
AUSTIN

I couldn't sleep. My thoughts kept circling back to the recent kill I'd made. The way my hands felt around the man's throat as his life essence was leeched away. It had felt so good, better than good. It was like staring down the barrel, facing the end, and walking away from it all ... *Better*. There was nothing comparable. I didn't know how Sam had resisted for as long as she did. I didn't even have a concept of what I was dealing with after I got her back from Malcolm.

I'd wanted to take her with me, for us to kill together, but she'd appeared so peaceful. And a part of me couldn't bear the thought of asking that of her, my beautiful Sam, to join me in the depths of depravity, to join me in death emotions. I wanted to protect her like I used to. To keep the darkness separate and away from her—away from our relationship.

Who the fuck am I kidding? Those days are gone, if they ever really existed.

I'd never been able to protect her. I'd done my best over the years and failed miserably. I hated admitting that to even myself, but she probably would have been better off with Nixon—the twisted fuck. I should have left her with him. If she never would have remembered who I was, and that Nixon wasn't her husband … but she couldn't let go of me any more than I could her.

Despair washed over me. I wanted to believe what I'd told her—that we deserved to be happy. Perhaps we did at one point, but not now.

At least I didn't.

Sam, my Sammy girl, she could still be safe. She could still come back from all of this. I'd made the right choice by trying to erase her memory of me when Cal had first taken me. She was too stubborn to forget that time though, plus our abilities were all tangled up together now. I couldn't seem to erase her mind when she had the same power, so to speak.

I leaned against the brick wall behind the shady dive bar. I wasn't sure where my head was anymore. I was confused more times than not, driven by something that felt extrinsic. I was a fucking fool to think that I could ever really have a life with Sam. People like me don't get happily-ever-afters, no matter how hard they try.

You should leave her, for her own good.

No! My entire being rebelled at the mere thought. Even if I somehow found the strength—I needed her.

Don't be selfish. You can't be saved. She can be.

Whirling around, I punched the brick wall, my hand exploding with pain. It focused me, centering me in the moment. Just then the man I'd been waiting for exited the bar. I'd originally planned on choking him to death, just like the other, but instead—

I let my bloody fist fly, cold cocking him. Not very dignified, but it wasn't meant to be a fight-starting blow. I wanted to kill him. I just wanted to get a little dirty first.

The man was thin, older, and he immediately crumpled to the ground. I paused a moment to pull my hoodie up over my head. I had the power to erase myself from whoever's mind that might see us, but I'd rather not have to bother. I rolled him over and began pummeling him with my fists, one after the other, over and over.

After a few minutes, the beating I was giving him began to push him into a more critical state. I slipped into feel his last emotions, and a smile spread across my face. The fact that he still thought he might survive—it was exhilarating when he finally realized he most likely wouldn't. By the time he took his last breath, a bloody and rattling one, I was soaring on a death high like I'd never felt before. I heard myself laugh, the sound dark and demented.

"Hey, man! What the fuck?" Someone had stepped out of the bar, and I'd been so engrossed I hadn't noticed.

I charged him, letting my hands settle around his throat. His eyes widened. I didn't register the new man's feature's and I didn't care, what mattered was my end game—another death. This time I went straight for the kill, strangling him with surprising ease. As I rifled through his mind … I paused a moment. He wasn't a criminal of any kind, just a blue-collar guy having a beer in a bar after work that was close to his home. He had a wife and kids that he treated well.

I started to step away … but couldn't. I didn't care anymore. I was numb to everything but my own needs. After all, it wasn't my fault that he was in the wrong place at the wrong time. Shit like that happened all the time. Bad luck for him, good luck for me.

I tightened my grip.

Exhaling with delight, my chest heaved with the exertion of having just killed two fully grown men with my bare hands. My mind flashed to Sam. I needed her—needed to be inside of her.

My gaze slid over the crumpled bodies in front of me. Something clicked. "No … I can't do this to her. I can't. I just can't." I stuffed my hands in my jacket pockets and hurried out of the alley. I loved Sam too much to make her into what I'd become. She could still be saved.

I was past salvation of any kind.

Chapter 27

SAM

"Going somewhere?" I narrowed my eyes at Austin as he approached where I'd been waiting for him.

His head snapped up, and he flinched away from me. "Sam? What the hell are you doing?"

"Not letting you do something completely asinine." I scowled. "Like leave me."

"H-How long have you been here? I didn't feel you nearby." He shifted uncomfortably, which pissed me off even more.

"Yeah, I know you didn't." I gritted my teeth, fighting the urge to smack him. "I've been here long enough."

It'd been one of the most difficult things I'd ever done not slipping in to enjoy the deaths with him. I could feel the energy of them wafting off of him in a tangible hum. I'd arrived too late and couldn't prevent his kills. So I'd done my best not to fall into the insanity—the much-desired insanity—with him.

Austin flipped his hood down, running his hands through his hair with agitation. "It's too late for me. We've been deluding ourselves. We're not going to get a happy ending, Sam. But maybe you can."

"Hell fucking no, you asshole. Do not pull that self-sacrificing bullshit that you tried to pull," I threw my hands up in the air, "one too many times. I'm done with it." I took a step closer to him. "It's you and me, Austin. You and me against the world. If you go down, then I go down, and vice versa."

Austin came at me in a rush, dropping down to press his face against my stomach as he wrapped his muscular arms around me. "I—" He swallowed a few times, choked up by his emotions. "I love you."

I rested my hand on his head, my heart squeezing. There was never any doubt that he loved me. He wouldn't even consider leaving me if he didn't, which was the rub. "We'll get through this together. No more changing your mind and trying to run off like a jackass."

His arms tightened around me, but he didn't move.

"Remember what you told me once—you told me that you'd love me no matter what and you'd do anything to keep me, even if it meant killing someone every day for me. Well …" I cupped the side of his face, forcing him to look up the line of my body at me. "Ditto."

His pupils dilated, but that was the only reaction he

gave me. His mind was currently closed off behind a rock-solid barrier.

"Now come on, we need to get out of here before the cops show up."

Austin slowly rose to his feet, and when I interlaced my fingers with his, he heaved a long, shaky breath before lumbering after me.

Chapter 28
NIXON

My gut churned as I watched Sam and Austin have their touching little moment. What she didn't realize was that she'd just saved his life. Temporarily at least. No matter how I did it, Sam would be heartbroken when I killed Austin, therefore I didn't want her to witness it if possible. Plus, she might do something stupid like retaliate against me. I couldn't steal Austin's abilities and make a run for it if I ended up dead. Sam was always predictably unpredictable, which made things difficult. Mainly because of her erratic behavior, my plan was precarious at best, the pieces fragile and dependent that I execute them in a certain way and order for me to be ultimately successful.

I would have to be patient and wait for the right moment, as much as it chafed to do so.

Fuck, fuck, fuck. My fists balled up at my sides. I yearned to rip her out of his grasp and to beat him to death just like he'd done to the man behind the bar. We used to be friends, Austin and me, but I was hard-pressed to remember how and why. Now the only redeeming quality I could conjure up was that he'd kept Sam alive at times when I couldn't.

"I've been waiting for you."

A chill ran up my spine as my own voice met my ears. I turned slowly, coming face to face with my twin. "Who the fuck are you?"

"Ultimately, it doesn't matter. I thought you might want these though." He handed me a large manila envelope. "Use them wisely." He winked, before turning to casually stride away while whistling a tune I couldn't quite place.

I glanced down at the folder and then back up in the direction Austin and Sam had just gone. I tucked the folder under my arm, heading after them. Being approached by the someone who had been masquerading as me was weird, but sadly being who I was … I'd seen weirder.

Chapter 29
SAM

I squeezed Austin's hand. "Nixon is following us," I whispered under my breath.

"Yeah, I'm aware."

"How do we want to handle it?" I kept my eyes forward, attempting to act natural. My muscles stiffened with the effort.

"I'm going to go down that alley up ahead on the right. I'll pretend to run from you. You stay put, and he'll come to you … guaranteed."

My chest tightened. Dealing with Nixon at the moment promised to be taxing to my already fragile state. "All right."

I let Austin's hand go. A few steps later, he took off at top speed down the alleyway. I feigned surprise, yelling after him, "Austin! What the hell are you doing?"

Just as he'd predicted, Nixon saw his opportunity and pounced, literally. He was behind me in an instant, his arms wrapped around my throat and waist, dragging me backwards.

"Don't fight me, Sam," he commanded, but of course I didn't obey. I had to make it believable, after all.

"Surprise, asshole!" Austin exclaimed with an edge of amusement mingled in with his anger. He wrenched Nixon away from me, and I stumbled around to face them. Austin already had Nixon by the throat.

"Wait! Stop! We need him alive!" I should have known Austin would go straight for the kill, and under the circumstances, I couldn't really blame him.

Austin reluctantly released Nixon's neck, and I pulled my handgun from the holster I had hidden at my back. "You have some explaining to do," I stated calmly, despite my rapid pulse.

Nixon drew in a few deep breaths, and meeting my gaze steadily he said, "Fine. I suppose I do."

"I DON'T KNOW what you're talking about," Nixon repeated with no less vehemence than he had the first few times we'd asked him. "I didn't kill anyone. You two are the ones who left the body in your hotel room. I assumed you two were the ones who killed her."

Nixon was on his knees in the center of the hotel room, his hands on the top of his head. I was sitting on the bed with my handgun pointed straight at him. His void shields were up tight. Otherwise, we could have just slipped in to get the information we needed.

Austin was chomping at the bit to kill Nixon, not that I blamed him, but I hated how bloodthirsty he'd become. I blamed myself. If I hadn't been so weak, my death addiction wouldn't have infected him with such severity. I despised myself for all of it.

"Just hand over the files," Austin growled.

Nixon reached into the back of his pants, producing a rolled-up folder. "Here. Take them. I have no idea what's in them though. I haven't had a chance to look them over."

"You're the one who wanted to steal them. How could you not know?"

Nixon's eyes narrowed to thin slits. "I told you, that wasn't me."

"Yeah, whatever," I snapped. "Cal's dead. He's the only one who could—"

"Obviously not," Nixon interjected. "Someone else is—"

Austin backhanded the side of his face. Nixon's words were swallowed by the motion, but he didn't cry out in pain or flinch, he merely spit blood and smiled. "You feel better now?"

Austin bared his teeth. "Not even close."

"Enough!" My voice crept up an octave, perilously close to being shrill. "We don't have time for this bullshit. Austin, we need to read those files."

After rising from the bed, I made my way over to scoop

up the folder, which was now on the floor in front of Nixon. I picked it up and backed away from him slowly, all the while watching Nixon as he tracked me with his dark gaze.

"You going to shoot me when you're done there?" Nixon's voice held a challenge.

I ground my teeth together, causing my molars to ache. "Maybe."

A deep, rumbling sound shook the hotel, causing my heart to thrash against my ribcage and pound against my eardrums. Everything went dark. I heard Austin swear, and then the floor vibrated under my feet. I couldn't see a damn thing and I didn't know what was going on. Dread settled in my stomach, and I knew we needed to act but I wasn't sure what to do.

"Austin?" I hated how my voice wavered with uncertainty.

"I'm right here. We need to get out of here. Now." Austin's voice grew closer to me as he spoke. When I felt his hands skim my arm, I threw myself into him, hugging him tightly.

The hotel door swung open, and dim lighting illuminated Nixon's large frame. "It's mighty peculiar that someone just so happens to be setting off some kind of explosives with you two here," Nixon said, sarcasm dripping from his tone.

"What's that supposed to mean?" I demanded.

"I think someone wants you both dead. You better come with me."

"Hell no," I immediately replied. "I don't trust you one little bit, as I'm sure you know."

"You can trust that I don't want you hurt, Sam." His gaze moved up to Austin. "You know that I would never hurt her."

"Okay. Temporary truce." Austin tensed around me, the words seemingly causing physical pain to say.

I bit my tongue, knowing it wasn't the time for arguments. We needed to react quickly. Plus, I did trust both Nixon and Austin with my life. Either of them wouldn't hesitate to die to protect me. And I was confident that Nixon didn't have anything to do with the explosion because he wouldn't risk my safety. It wasn't much on the trust scale, but under the circumstances, it was going to have to do.

I squeezed Austin's hand once and nodded at Nixon. "All right, let's go."

The three of us made our way cautiously from our room on the tenth floor. Nixon led the way, me close at his heels, with Austin bringing up the rear. It hadn't escaped my notice that they had instinctively sandwiched me in the middle to provide me with the utmost safety. We obviously chose to use the stairs since, even if it worked, an elevator would be a bad idea. There could be an aftershock or something.

The trek down the stairs was uneventful until we reached the third floor. That was where we hit a bit of a snag. We were completely blocked off because of a collapse.

"Let's head back up to the fourth floor, we can try to get out one of the windows," Austin said as he eyed the rubble.

"We better move fast before—"

The hotel shook again, pieces of wall and ceiling raining down on us. "Run!" Austin shouted. He picked me up, throwing me over his shoulder as he took off up the stairs. The lights wavered, and I felt like I was on some kind of movie-themed amusement park ride. Somehow, we managed to get to the fourth floor unharmed with me slung over Austin's shoulder.

"End of the hall, the door's open." Nixon gestured wildly at an open hotel room.

Austin followed Nixon, finally dropping me to my feet once inside of the room. Him and Nixon immediately went to work on the window. "How are we getting down? We're on the fourth floor."

Both men ignored me or didn't hear me because they were so focused. They worked together in a manner that showcased the fact that they used to be friends. Neither one of them said a word, but they each knew what the other wanted and needed with the task at hand. I paced nervously, not knowing what to do.

With one last grunt of exertion, the window was pushed away. I wasn't sure how they'd managed since hotel windows are made to not ... well, break.

Nixon leaned out to get a look before he addressed Austin. "I'll shimmy down the side, get to the awning, and then you send her down." Austin silently agreed, and Nixon climbed out the window.

"Sam," Austin said. "Your turn."

"I don't trust him. Maybe you should—"

"I need you safe."

Meeting his panicked gaze, I nodded. "Fine."

Just as I stepped out the window, another explosion shook the building. I clung to the bricks by sheer will alone. My fingers cramped and began to turn white. I knew I wouldn't be able to hold—

"Sam!" Austin shouted as I lost my grip.

I felt weightless for a moment, and then all went dark.

Chapter 30

SAM

"Chloe, wake up!" I flinched as someone tapped my forehead with what felt like a finger. "You need to wake up." A very aggressive finger.

"I'm not," my eyes fluttered open, "that's not my name anymore. I'm—" My mouth gaped, and the ability to speak was temporarily lost to me. Standing right in front of me … was me.

The other me grinned. "No, you're Chloe. I'm Samantha."

I shook my head in bewilderment. "This has to be a dream." Or I cracked my head—really, really hard.

"Don't worry, it's a dream. But that doesn't mean what I have to tell you isn't extremely important."

Feeling somewhat mollified since I knew I was only dreaming and not, in fact, insane, or leaking brain matter, I relaxed a bit. "Okay, spit it out then."

"Alrighty. Try to keep up because I'm about to drop

some seriously disturbing shit on you. Shit that you most likely won't be able to handle."

"You don't know that," I snapped.

Samantha quirked an eyebrow. "Actually, I do because otherwise, I wouldn't exist."

I crossed my arms over my chest. "You don't exist. This is a dream."

"Ever hear of split personalities? Well, dear Chloe, you're pretty much there. Or I should say we." She motioned back and forth between us with her hand.

My eyes widened and I gulped convulsively. "No, I would know. That doesn't make sense." And yet, it kind of did. Hadn't the same idea crossed my mind not too long ago? I wondered about how I'd really chosen my secondary name, and if part of the purpose of my and Austin's torture was to force split personalities upon us. It had seemed very plausible and actually made a lot of sense, but then I'd just pushed the concept away. Had I stumbled upon the truth but been too much in denial? Or perhaps I really couldn't handle it?

"Listen, you had some royally fucked-up shit done to you as a child. Most couldn't handle what they made you do. I don't blame you. But that's how I came about. I'm the part of your personality that does what needs to be done to survive. You—*Chloe*—couldn't handle it. Now, granted, the things done to you were meant to cause this division of personality. It was part of the experiment or conditioning, or whatever you want to call it. I prefer the term torture, personally. Bottom line … They wanted me to exist so they could control me. They'll never be able to. Split personality doesn't translate to compliance, especially in my case."

I inhaled a shaky breath. She'd answered all of my questions like I'd spoken them out loud. As much as I didn't want to believe Samantha, her … my words rang true within me. "But I never lost pieces of time or—"

Samantha lifted her eyebrows and smirked, her expression immediately derailing my train of thought. The memories of me being forced to kill animals when I was younger sprung into my mind. "I didn't remember parts of my childhood until recently. Despite the fact that—"

"Yep, you had all of your memories returned. Just not all of *ours.*" Samantha sat down across from me, her legs folded up beneath her. "You haven't needed me in a very long time, but you do now."

"So the dual name thing, it means more than I thought. Austin?"

"Austin is in the same boat as you, or I should say Alex. The thing is, Austin has been running the show for a while now. I can tell."

I didn't know what to think of that. Alex and Austin were the same person, weren't they? I was both Chloe and Samantha, and yet I was having a conversation with myself like we were two separate people. "Why are you here?" I demanded.

"Like I said, you need me. Besides, Austin and I work very well together. You do better with Alex."

I huffed out a frustrated breath. "We're the same people."

Samantha leaned back, twirling a piece of hair around her finger. "One day I hope that can be true again. All of us, me and you, does love all of Austin and Alex, you were right about that when you considered it before. That's also why it works so perfectly. After all this shit is dealt with, I hope we can just be … normal." A wistful expression settled onto Samantha's face. "For now, you need to let me take control."

"So you get to be privy to all of my actions and thoughts, but I don't even remember when you're in control? Wait … You need my permission?"

She rolled her eyes. "Apparently I do need your permission now. I didn't used to. I had control for a few minutes back when you were being held prisoner. I'm the one who got you out, and then *poof* you took over again. Then uncertainty and waffling abounded. Good thing Austin showed up when he did."

"But I remember all of that. I didn't blank out or—"

"We're bleeding together, I think. That's why I can talk to you now. But I still need to be the one in control for what's coming. You need to let me. Chloe," Samantha leaned forward, her eyes boring into mine, "we need to save them … Austin and Alex. And we need to save ourselves."

I stared at myself, which was a bit disconcerting doing it without a mirror. I thought about all the revelations I'd recently had while I was a captive, and the memories of my torture as a child. I considered how bad off Austin was with his addiction, and how close to the edge I was. "You really think you can save all of us?"

Samantha smirked, her expression eerily similar to one that Austin would give me in that situation. "I know I can."

"Okay." I shrugged, unsure of how to give her the go-ahead. "I give you my permission to take control?" It came out more of a question than a statement though.

Samantha snorted. "Good enough."

I bit my lower lip with uncertainty. "Which one of us is more addicted to the death emotions?" I maybe should have asked that little question first before giving my permission.

"Me, of course. I don't feel the guilt like you do." She grinned at me. "Austin and I are going to have so much fun."

Alarm bells went off in my head. "Wait! I thought you were going to save us?"

"I am. But I'm going to do it my way."

Shit. What did I just do? Shouldn't a person at least be able to trust themselves?

Chapter 31
SAM

"Sam, can you hear me? Sam?" Austin's voice wound into my ear from close by.

"She's still not responding. I'm taking her to the hospital," Nixon growled.

"No, you're not. She's fine. She doesn't have a concussion. She didn't even hit her head."

"Then explain to me what the fuck happened."

"I don't know, she passed out before you even caught her. I saw it. She's going to wake up fine. You pretending to take her to the hospital isn't going to work."

"I'm not fucking pretending—"

"Shut up," I rasped. "Can the two of you not argue for five minutes?" I opened my eyes slowly, focusing on Austin. My heart swelled at the sight of him. We'd made it out of yet another life-and-death situation. That was a reason to celebrate the way we did best.

I locked my hands around the back of his neck, pulling

him to me. As soon as he was close enough, I slanted my lips over his, plunging my tongue into his mouth. He immediately responded with equal if not more fervor.

"Stop! Just fucking stop!" Nixon bellowed.

Austin pulled away just in time for me to see Nixon dash out of the front door of our new location—what appeared to be a fresh hotel room, or at least one in a building that wasn't being blown to smithereens.

"You should—"

"Doesn't matter. We have the files and we can always kill him later." Austin's blue eyes sizzled with lust, the heat from them burning me from the inside out.

I didn't respond verbally, just ensnared his lips with mine again. Our tongues intertwined, and I reveled in the taste of Austin—it was always sharper after almost losing him. Everything was more acute after a near-death experience, that's why the death addiction was so potent.

Austin groaned as my hands roamed over his body to land on his perfectly formed, muscular ass. *God, I love his ass. It really is perfect.* I wanted to feel it moving and bunching while he pounded me towards bliss. His clothes needed to come off immediately.

"Austin." I didn't need to say anything else. Uttering his name was a benediction and a plea rolled into one.

He groaned deep in the back of his throat, tearing at my clothes. I lifted myself up and returned the favor.

Once we were both naked, he pressed the lower half of his body into mine, pinning me, but not entering quite yet. His rock-hard cock slid through my slick folds, sending tremors up my spine. He leaned in, capturing my eyes with his darkening gaze. One hand moved to encircle my neck, and his pupils dilated, causing his eyes to appear almost black. Most women would have been afraid, especially knowing how he'd strangled multiple people to death. But not me, I trusted him implicitly. Austin would never hurt me. He loved me. Nothing could ever change that.

I arched my pelvis up, meeting his gaze with both confidence and love, even as his fingers tightened around my throat. "Fuck me," I commanded, delighting in the near-perfect sensation of him slipping home inside of me.

"I love you," he rasped, tightening his fingers even more.

I sucked in a ragged breath, the limited oxygen causing spots to dance in front of my eyes. Austin slid one of his hands down my body, lifting my leg over his shoulder, the other hand moved up my neck to get a better grip. After each thrust, he ground his pelvis against me and squeezed my throat during the duration of his movement. My focus narrowed down to sensation alone. Everything was Austin and what he was doing to my body. He owned me like he never had before. I loved every second of it.

My eyes slammed shut as my orgasm took me by surprise, yanking me off into oblivion without the slightest bit of warning. Austin's grip tightened around my throat to the point where I couldn't breathe, but only for a moment, a moment in which my entire body exploded, prolonging the pleasure I'd already been experiencing.

Austin's fingers loosened when he pulled out to come all over me. I opened my eyes, sputtering for oxygen, and watched as Austin peered down at me in awe.

"You've never looked so beautiful." He leaned forward, running his index finger along my neck before trailing it down through the valley of my breasts. "You're probably going to bruise."

"I don't care," I croaked.

Austin grinned, showcasing his gloriously sexy dimple. "You really are perfect for me, you know that, right? No matter what I want, you'll give it to me."

"Just like you'll give me anything I want."

His expression turned serious, all traces of his lighter mood gone. "Anything. You know I'd do anything for you. This life—nothing … it all means nothing without you. I want to share everything with you."

We were absolutely on the same page, as usual. "Yes, everything together. You and me. But first, we have to take care of business."

Austin lay down on top of me, not caring that we would both get sticky. We could clean up in the shower together. "I like the way you think."

I shoved my fingers into his hair, tugging lightly. "You and me against the world. Always."

"My good Sammy girl," Austin murmured against my skin. "You and me forever. Nothing will ever change that. I'll make sure of it."

Chapter 32
NIXON

It had taken everything—and I do mean *everything*—inside of me not to kill Austin right then and there with my bare hands. Forced to watch the way the two of them just started groping each other like I wasn't even there was ... was—

"Fuck!" I punched the wall, grimacing at the stab of pain.

He's probably balls deep inside of her right now and she doesn't even care that I'm hurting. Knowing how many times the two of them had been together. Knowing ... just knowing—

"Fuck!" I bellowed again.

I took in several deep breaths, trying to let them calm me. *Stop thinking about it. When Austin's dead he'll be out of the picture for good. And then I'll have the rest of my life to fuck away all remnants of his filthy touch from my Sam. It'll be like he never existed. For her at least. I won't be as lucky since I'll never be able to purge his presence from my brain. I'll never be able to forget the way she looked at him when—*

Fuck. I wish I could forget her. Move on.

I yanked at my hair in frustration. I'd tried so many times to forget her, to leave her in my past. But there was some inexplicable thing that kept me coming back—something about her that I'd never not want, crave. It was her or no one for me, a sad truth I'd adjusted my life around.

Okay, enough of the pity party. Think, think, think ... you need to adjust your plan, figure out the next step.

I'd thought it was going to be so easy: track them down, kill Austin, and disappear with Sam forever.

And yet I'd hesitated at the hotel. *Why? Why the fuck did I hesitate?*

The more I considered it, the more sense it would have made to do it then. I could have killed him in the mayhem and wiped Sam's memory of the entire ordeal. That was the plan from the beginning, and I'd choked. Plus, I'd forced myself not to follow through.

Groaning, I shook my head. It just didn't make sense. Why the hell would I do that? Something didn't feel right.

Or was that just another rationalization? Sam had always been my weakness. Perhaps I didn't want to burn the memory of her temporary hatred into my mind from when I killed Austin. It was something I'd never forget even if she did.

Yes, that has to be it. There isn't another feasible explanation.

But no matter, there was no use in crying over split milk. I missed one chance, so therefore I'd just have to create another. I'd resume following them and wait for the next opportunity. Because it would come, and I would be there waiting.

Chapter 33

IMPOSTER NIXON

I wanted to bang my head against the wall. The fact that I'd been forced to slip into the real Nixon's mind to keep him from killing Austin had been torture. Because I wanted Austin dead, so fucking much. But on my schedule. After all, I didn't spend the ridiculous amount of time planning everything just to have Nixon ruin it for me now. Besides, he'd be tormented enough after Sam's death. I almost felt sorry for the dumb fuck. And maybe a little for Sam, too. Both her and Nixon were merely collateral damage. My real goal was to make Austin suffer for what he'd done.

It had taken me years, and finally, things were lining up the way I wanted. I couldn't and wouldn't allow some small blunder to ruin my perfect revenge. Not only was Nixon a constant problem that I had to consider, but his idiot of a mother, too. She'd been the one who'd ordered the attack on the hotel they'd all been in. Even though

Nixon was her son, she considered his death acceptable. *Poor bastard.* I knew what it was like to grow up with such a cold-hearted bitch for a mother … after all, she'd given birth to me as well. I supposed the apple didn't fall far from the tree in my case, since I was a complete sociopath just like her. I'd stop at nothing to get what I wanted, no matter who got hurt.

And what I wanted more than anything was my revenge against Austin.

Chapter 34
SAM

I was late again.

I hefted my shoulder bag and prayed I hadn't forgotten anything I needed for class. I was behind schedule because of my student aid job, which was beyond ridiculous because you would think of all people, they'd understand punctuality when it came to their student workers. I hated being late, especially for my Sociology 101 class. I thought it would be an easy A, but—

"Hey!" I exclaimed as someone slammed into me from behind, forcing me to the ground. I scrambled to get up, but whoever it was weighed a ton. Something sticky was leaking down my back.

"Someone's shooting from The Cathedral!" a male voice yelled in panic.

"Oh my God!" I gasped as the words combined with my current situation sank in. I decided to remain where I was on

the ground for the time being. I had a sick feeling that I knew what was on me now.

It could have been me. Tears erupted from my eyes. I didn't want to die. I eased my arms out from under me and laid perfectly still.

A feminine scream sounded close to me, a body thudding right next to where I was lying. I turned my head and saw a girl trying to drag herself across the pavement. She'd been shot in the shoulder it looked like, which meant she still had a chance if she didn't draw attention to herself. It didn't even look like she was bleeding all that bad. She might even be saved before she bled out if she didn't keep doing what she was doing.

She swiveled her head in my direction and locked gazes with me. "Fifteen," she whispered, saliva pulling at the corners of her mouth. "Fift—"

Another shot rang out and pieces of her brain hit me in the face.

"Nooo ..." I breathed, squeezing my eyes tightly shut. I didn't want to die. I just wanted to be on time for class. I—

"Sam. Wake up," Austin gently commanded.

"Shit," I muttered, running my hands through my sweat-dampened hair. "Not again."

"What the hell was that all about? It didn't feel like a vision, but it most definitely wasn't a normal dream."

I grimaced. I hated when Austin just slipped into my mind and started barraging me with follow-up questions before I even had a chance to figure out the details for myself. "I really don't know. I've been having dreams, or nightmares, all different, but all with someone saying *fifteen* in every single one. It makes absolutely no sense to me. It feels important though."

"Hmm," he grunted, as I felt him slip into my mind to delve into the other dreams with the same pattern. After a moment he met my gaze with bewilderment of his own. "They don't make any sense."

Sitting up, I scanned the room. Frustration at not knowing what was going on with my dreams morphed into motivation to get answers in other areas. "It doesn't matter right now. We need to figure out what's so important in those files, and we need to—"

"I read them while you were sleeping."

I narrowed my eyes at Austin and crossed my arms over my chest. "Of course you did." I'd say unbelievable but of course it wasn't at all. "So care to share the old-fashioned way, or do you want to just let me, you know?" I tapped my fingertips along my temple.

"Probably easier to just show you." He pushed the information into my mind without any further preamble.

The files contained information about the program Jake had mentioned to me, Project Reaper. Inside were all the birth names and background information on every person that had ever been a part of the program, dating back to the first 'recruits', the group that Austin and I had been part of. It also told us what had been done to each person and what the hopeful outcome had been.

Apparently, I'd been right. Austin and I had been part of a failed experiment, one that was supposed to splinter off our personalities to form the perfect assassins. The second deadly personality would only activate upon command, leaving our other side completely clueless. And we were supposed to work together as a team. Not just us, but everyone in the experiment was paired off as well. To make it easier, Natalie and David had simply tried to strengthen any natural bonds like what had sprung up between Austin and me.

There had been one more experiment done to us though. They wanted to see what would happen if one of the bonded pair died. Would they be able to bond with someone else? Obviously, they hadn't killed Austin, but they'd tried to forge the same kind of relationship between me and another boy, his name was Jase. The results: Jase had bonded with me, but all I'd wanted was Alex.

I had one guess who Jase had grown up to be.

"Nixon," I said out loud.

"Yeah, that's exactly what I was thinking."

"I wonder if he knows?"

"It doesn't matter, Sam."

Biting my lower lip, I thought about Nixon. He'd tried time after time to rip me away from Austin. He'd been relentless in his pursuit of me. With everything else in his life, he'd always seemed so stable, so reasonable, all except when it came to me. Austin was right, it didn't really matter why he was the way he was, but at least I had answers now. "Okay, so what do we do with the rest of the information? It really doesn't do us any good."

Austin slid up next to me and hauled me into his lap.

He wrapped his arms around me, and I rested my cheek against his shoulder. "That's what I thought at first, but then I realized that the answers we're searching for have to be somewhere with the people on that list. Which means we need to track down every last one of them."

I puffed out a long sigh. "I don't know what we're doing anymore, Austin. I think we should just go kill everyone back at the compound. Basically, we should kill everyone that knows anything about us, and then we can start fresh lives somewhere else. Hopefully somewhere tropical."

"My good Sammy girl." I could hear the smile in Austin's voice. "I was getting to that part. Great minds think alike and all that bullshit." He chuckled. "Once we track down all the people on that list, once we get any and all information that we can from them … we kill them. We're going to tie up any loose ends out there. Then we'll take care of Natalie and her little gang. There won't be anyone left to come after us when we're done. We won't need to run to someplace off the grid unless we want to …" Austin's voice trailed off for a moment before he seemed to refocus. "I'm going to give you the life you want, Sam. I'm going to get it all for you—for *us*."

I pressed my face tighter into Austin, a smile tugging at my lips. I was suddenly optimistic about our future, Austin's determination catchy. "We can enjoy all those deaths together. It'll be like one last hurrah before we settle down to a normal kind of life."

"Mmmm hmmm," Austin murmured against my hair

as his fingers danced along my spine. "But first I'm thinking that I need to fuck you just one more time before we set off on our little adventure."

He flipped me onto my back, and I squealed with delight. Austin was the one thing that could distract me from the outside world indefinitely and I was happy to let him.

Chapter 35
SAM

"Lucky for us, the majority of them all settled around Pittsburgh so we won't have very far to go," I stated, watching the blur of colors race by me from inside the SUV.

"I don't think luck has anything to do with it. Something like that is not a coincidence."

"So they were kept or placed here? Maybe drawn to each other?"

"Either one, maybe both, or something else entirely. I just know it's definitely not a coincidence."

I agreed. What were the chances, really? There were thirty people on the list. Many of them were already marked as deceased. Of the fourteen who remained alive, every single one of them were living in or around the greater Pittsburgh area. Too freaky to be anything accidental. "What if Natalie catches onto our plan before we're ready?"

Austin's hands whitened on the steering wheel. "Let her try and stop us," he grated. "Now that we're together, nothing can."

I reached over and intertwined my fingers with Austin's. Just touching him made me feel stronger. What he said was true—every time we'd been at our most vulnerable was when we'd been separated. Now that we were together, I was sure we were about as close to unbeatable as they came.

Tapping my foot anxiously, I squeezed Austin's hand once more before letting go of it. I was wired. Excitement about kicking off our plan was coursing through my system. We were going to get our lives back. So what if a bunch of people were going to die in the process? Not only was the world that Austin and I lived in weird, but in cases like these it was Darwinism at its best. Thankfully we were at the top of the food chain, which was why everyone either wanted to use and control us or kill us.

My inner musings were cut short when the SUV pulled to a smooth stop in a residential area. "We here?"

Austin's gaze was fixated in the rearview mirror. "Almost, but Nixon is following us again."

"What?" I exclaimed, twisting around in my seat. Sure enough, I got a glimpse of Nixon in the driver's seat of a silver car as it veered off down a side street. "He's losing his touch. Or he doesn't care if we know that he's on our tail."

"He's just being reckless. He cares." The muscles in Austin's jaw ticked with tension.

"So we know he's there. Big deal," I huffed. "Does it effect our plans?"

"No. It doesn't. It's just that—" Austin slammed his fist against the steering wheel. "I want him dead."

"I'm pretty sure the feeling is mutual, which is why we need to be extra careful."

At some point I would have felt guilt at the idea of Nixon being dead. Once he'd been a friend, and we'd lived for years as husband and wife. There was no denying that I'd harbored a special kind of soft spot for him. I couldn't love him the way he wanted, even if Austin wasn't in the picture, but I'd wished him happiness with someone else. Now ... well, now he was just another obstacle standing in between me and my happiness with Austin.

"He's not going to get the jump on me," Austin snapped, as if the very idea was an insult to him.

"Okaaay," I drawled, not wanting to delve into the conversation any deeper at the moment. It would only serve to distract and delay us, and I was ready to get to our destination. I was beyond ready to get to our destination. Sensing my feelings on the matter, I'm sure since I was broadcasting them loud and clear to Austin, kind of like a mental shout, he shifted into drive and peeled out of our parked spot, the tires squealing. I resisted the urge to roll my eyes. *Men.*

We drove for about five minutes before he turned quickly to the right and maneuvered us up a long driveway, hopping out of the SUV as soon as the engine was off.

His anticipation and excitement hummed along my nerve endings. I outstretched my senses as we made our way up the front walkway to the house. It was a small, brick row home, old but well kept, and a lot nicer than the similar ones surrounding it. It was obvious that the occupant took pride in their possessions.

"Who lives here? Which one is it again?" I whispered from the side of my mouth, not breaking my gaze away from the front door as we drew closer.

Austin took my hand within his and squeezed. "Joanna Donay. Empath."

"Hmm …" I grunted. A woman. Most of the people that were still alive on the list were men. I wasn't sure what that meant, and I didn't care aside from idly noting the fact, and wondering if it had any kind of importance.

We paused at the front door. It was a deep red color, shiny, with no peeling paint or cracks. I normally didn't notice those kinds of details, but it was just so perfect somehow that it stood out to me.

"Here we go," I murmured.

My finger shook slightly as I reached out, pressing the doorbell. The chimes echoed inside of the house. Footsteps reverberated loudly, heels clicking on hardwood or linoleum floors. The door swung smoothly open to reveal a tall blonde woman with pale skin. She was probably in her mid-thirties, looking like she stepped right off the set of some retro TV show, like *Mad Men* or something. She was even wearing a frilly apron, as if she'd been cooking, and cooking in heels to boot. I fought to keep from blatantly staring.

Austin fell right into his charming act, smiling brightly at her. "Hi, Joanna. We're here to—"

She smiled tightly at us. "I know why you're here." She stepped out of the way to let us in.

I met her gaze, my eyes widening with surprise.

"I've been waiting for something like this for a long time now. And last night I had a dream about you two. I know you've come for answers … and to kill me."

"Being anything beyond an empath wasn't in your files," I blurted out, still a bit off-kilter from her laissez-faire attitude about … everything, especially her imminent death.

"No, I'm not. It felt like someone sent it to me." She closed the door softly behind us.

Austin tilted his head, studying her. "Why didn't you run?"

Joanna's lips pressed together in a thin line, her features pinched with annoyance. "I'm tired of running. I'm tired of always looking over my shoulder. I just want it all to end."

She turned to lead us down the narrow hallway into the kitchen, where the aroma of freshly baked pastries filled the air. "I bake when I'm nervous," she muttered, slightly chagrined. "I may be ready for this all to be over, but I'm afraid …"

"We'll make it quick for you," Austin offered. "Painless."

I felt the disappointment in him acutely. There was no point in making Joanna suffer, we wouldn't get the kind of death emotions from her that we wanted, not with her being prepared and at peace with the whole situation. My mood had taken a bit of a dive from that realization as well.

Joanna nodded at Austin as she nibbled her bottom lip. Her gaze roamed over him with appreciation. "The two of you a couple?"

I gritted my teeth, her lustful emotions aimed at him surging through me. Did she actually think that Austin might be willing to fuck her before he killed her?

"Yes," I snapped, wringing my hands, trying to not strangle her. "He's mine. I mean, he's my husband."

Austin wrapped his arm around my waist, tugging me into his side. "*You know I think it's extremely hot when you get jealous*," he whispered in my mind.

Joanna's eyes widened at my hostility. "Sorry. I meant no disrespect. I … well, I—" Her cheeks bloomed with color. "I just thought that if he was single—last request and all."

Austin smiled, showcasing his dimple, causing her to blush even more. "It's fine."

"*Is not*," I hissed directly into his mind.

He ignored my comment and addressed Joanna again. "You know why we're here, so …"

She pulled out a chair and sat down, folding her hands demurely in her lap. "Yes, I had a dream about you coming, like I said. I'll answer anything I can."

"Tell us what you know about Project Reaper," Austin requested, anticipation causing him to fidget.

"All right. It's not much, or I'd probably already be dead. Or if I was a stronger empath, I'd still be useful and—"

"Why aren't you dead?" The words just tumbled from my mouth.

"They want to see if I develop the addiction on my own. I haven't. They think all of us are stupid, like we don't know what's going on. We've all—all of us that were in the program—we all became quite adept at playing stupid. We had to if we wanted to survive."

"The death addiction?" Austin pulled away from me, sliding into the chair across from Joanna at her table.

I leaned against the wall and crossed my arms.

"Mhmm … All of us empaths have been their little obsession. Everyone else in the program, Project Reaper, the ones with different abilities, they were never as important as the empaths. They were just supporting characters, so to speak."

"Because they felt we'd make the perfect assassins."

Joanna lifted both of her perfectly arched brows to her hairline. "Exactly."

Austin snorted. "No denials will be coming from me."

I pushed off the wall and started to pace. "But we already knew all of this. Give us something we don't know."

Joanna shrugged. "I'm sorry, that's all I know, which is probably why they didn't kill me. I'm not a security risk."

Frustration boiled up within me. I snagged Austin's gaze as I moved past him. "Then what's the point of our little quest if no one knows anything that we don't already?"

"We're cleaning out the program, tying up loose ends, making sure there's no one left to send after us." Austin stood quickly, causing his chair to clatter to the ground. In one lightning-fast move, he'd rounded the table and had Joanna by the throat, but instead of the slow strangulation I was expecting—he wrenched her head to the side, cracking her neck. He was a man of his word. He told her he'd make it quick, and if not completely painless, it would have been pretty damn close.

Joanna's vacant eyes stared lifelessly at me, and Austin placed her body gently on the floor. He picked up a chocolate chip cookie from the table and stuffed it in his mouth. "Want one?" he asked while chewing.

"They do smell delicious."

"We'll take some for the road then." Austin rummaged through drawers and came out with some aluminum foil for our food plunder.

I picked up what looked like a sugar cookie and took a small bite. It was absolute perfection. The round wafer practically melted on my tongue. "She was a fantastic cook."

I was well aware that we should have been feeling guilt, remorse, regret—something other than what we were. After all, we'd just killed Joanna in cold blood and then helped ourselves to her baked goods. I just couldn't drum up the emotions though. Her death meant nothing to me. She was just a name on a list that we'd checked off. I knew she was a living, breathing person, but somehow it just didn't feel that way. The only person that mattered to me was Austin.

"You ready?" Austin met my gaze, his baby blues sparkling.

"Yeah. One down and thirteen more to go."

Chapter 36
IMPOSTER NIXON

Smiling to myself, I watched Sam and Austin walk back to their SUV. They seemed happy, and perfectly content with having just killed poor Joanna. I had actually kind of liked her. Not enough to care that she was dead, but enough to send her the vision of what her future held.

Maybe I'd done it a little for myself as well. I didn't want Sam and Austin to enjoy themselves too much, after all. By taking away the surprise element to Joanna's death, I took away the enjoyment that they would feel. Back in the beginning it didn't matter what kind of death it was, the addiction would have been fed to some small degree, but not now. Now they were both like me, they needed bigger and better to get the same level of high. Things were finally back on track with my plans. I just had to sit back and wait for things to come to fruition.

Chapter 37

NIXON

I had the same vision again, the one of Sam dying in my arms. I was almost positive now that it wasn't actually me. It was whoever was pretending to be me—my imposter. The whole thing had me on edge. It meant that nothing had changed. Despite my involvement, we were all still on the same course to our crash destination.

I have to get Sam away from Austin before it's too late.

I scrolled through my contact list, hitting send when I found the number I was searching for. "Yeah, I need a clean-up crew."

Once I'd shared the specifics of what needed to be done, I hung up. Natalie didn't want any interference from the media. We didn't need the publicity of another serial killer on the loose, especially one in Pittsburgh. Sure, if Sam got arrested, we could get her out, but no one wanted to deal with it. Plus, I, of course, wanted the path of least resistance between me disappearing with Sam for good.

I gave one last look at the pretty dead blonde on the floor before turning to leave the house. Natalie had provided me with the names that had been on the list. Instead of following Austin and Sam to their next victim, I'd simply choose one and wait them out. The time for all of this to end was finally near.

Chapter 38
SAM

Trepidation settled into my gut. It seemed like there was always something bad lurking just around the corner for Austin and me these days. It was only a matter of time before we ran headlong into the next problem.

Fidgeting in my seat, I eyed Austin who was being suspiciously quiet. It was the easier path to just slip into his mind, but it was more respectful to do things the normal way.

"What has you looking so pensive?" I asked while continuing to study his profile. It was unfair how attractive he was. I'd gotten over my insecurities a long time ago, at least when it came to other women. Even after all the years we'd been together, he still caused my stomach to twist with excitement just being near him, leaving me to wonder why he continued to choose me time and time again.

"Well, now I'm thinking about pulling over and doing you right here, right now." His voice dropped an octave, rumbling deliciously low. "How about it? Wanna fuck right here, right now?"

Batting my eyelashes, I smirked. "How can a girl say no to such an eloquently spoken offer?"

Austin swerved to the side of the road, tires squealing as he slammed on the brakes. He lunged over the center console, reaching for me. I flattened myself against the window, pretending to be afraid. Really, I was trying not to laugh or melt into a pile of oversexed goo. I did both.

"Yeah, you won't be laughing in a minute," Austin rasped.

He pulled me under him, sliding his hand up the back of my thigh to squeeze my ass. I arched up to grind my hot center against him. "We need to make this a quickie," I muttered, wishing it wasn't necessary, but we were on the side of the road. It wouldn't be long before someone would stop to see if we needed help. If we weren't in such a precarious position, Austin could just make us invisible, but then we'd run the very real risk of someone plowing into us.

"I suppose I can manage." Austin nipped at my earlobe and popped the button on my jeans with one finger.

"I thought you—" His lips stole my words.

Austin was all I thought about for the next ten minutes, give or take a few.

After we were finished and our clothes were all back in

their proper places, we continued on our journey to the next person on our list.

"DÉJÀ-VU," I muttered.

We'd arrived at our destination, and the house we were currently staring at was eerily similar to Joanna's, at least in its overall feel. It also had a perfectly painted red door. It caught my attention just like it had at Joanna's.

"It's just a door, Sam. Lots of people have red doors. They're actually quite popular."

"You're just saying that to make me feel better. Don't tell me it isn't creepy."

Austin sighed heavily. "It's a bit odd, but not creepy." He ran his hand through his hair, causing it to stick up in different directions. I had to stifle the urge to run my fingers through it.

I pursed my lips and willed my erratic heartbeat to slow down. "Okay, let's get this over with. Hopefully it goes better than round one with Joanna. By the way, who is this one?"

"Carlos Russell, also an empath."

"Yeah, I kind of figured after what Joanna said. I bet every single one on that list is some level of empath."

Austin grunted as he pulled himself out of the SUV. I followed suit, trailing along behind him up to the front door. I let him ring the doorbell.

A bullet punched through the door, narrowly missing

Austin's head. He swore, yanking me to the ground before I could react. Another few rounds of bullets sailed past us, but the shooter was aiming high. He obviously didn't have a ton of experience with taking out targets, lucky for us.

Something in me snapped. Maybe it was the fact that Austin and I were in life-or-death danger ... yet again. Or maybe it was something more. But suddenly, it was as if all of the guilt, trepidations ... just everything from the last couple of days were dumped over me like a bucket of ice water. My mind latched onto an image of Joanna's wide, lifeless eyes staring at me as I happily chomped on one of her cookies.

We'd just killed her—just killed her and walked away like her life had meant nothing. So what if she'd been ready for us? It didn't matter that she'd been tired of waiting for the other shoe to drop because of the Reaper Program. *Every life is precious. Every single life ...*

My mind drudged up another memory:

"Samantha, kill it."

In front of me, in a small wire cage, was a black and white floppy-eared bunny. It was so tiny it could have fit in the palm of my hand. Its tiny pink nose twitched at me.

"I can't." I bit down on my lower lip so hard I tasted the coppery tang of my blood. "And why do you keep calling me Samantha? My name," I choked out, "is Chloe."

And then I'd killed it. I'd just snapped its little neck. It'd been alive one minute and I'd just stolen it—its life. I'd stolen so many lives. Taken them without the slightest twinge. And Austin, the two of us together ... how could we do such terrible things to people when we loved each other so completely?

Something was wrong … extremely wrong.

And I knew why.

The answer was within a memory, just beyond my reach. *It's all just too much. Too much.* I clutched my head, digging my fingers into my scalp, and let loose an anguished wail.

I want out. I need out. I can't do it anymore, any of it. I just can't do it. I'm tainted. I can feel it moving inside of me. It's like the sludge I found in Malcolm's mind. But now it's thriving inside of me. Like a parasite feeding off of me, living only because I let it.

My vision faltered. "Get it out," I heard myself say. "Get it out. It's everywhere. It's— Get it out of me!" I tore at my skin, my chest compressing as if someone was sitting on it, and I struggled to breathe. "Austin … please *help* me," I choked out.

"Sam. I'm here. I'm here. I'll fix it. I'll make it right." His cool fingers skimmed along my temples, but no reprieve found me just yet. Fortunately, when he managed to press me mentally to sleep, I didn't fight, and I was swept away into oblivion, leaving my new hell behind.

Chapter 39

AUSTIN

"Sam. Sammy? God, please … just please." I had absolutely no idea what triggered her, but I'd seen it before. When Sam had slipped into Malcolm's mind when she was untrained and unready, she'd reacted the same way. But I'd been able to help her before, and now there was an impenetrable wall preventing me from doing a damned thing.

We'd barely made it off of that porch without getting shot. Besides helping Sam, I wanted nothing more than to go back and take care of Carlos. I wouldn't give him a quick and easy death like Joanna, not after he'd almost killed my wife.

Sam flailed around on the small, dingy motel bed, her face scrunched up with a mixture of terror and confusion. I thought that if I took her somewhere private, I could fix it, just like I'd done before.

I'd been wrong.

I don't know what to fucking do.

"Sam ..." I smoothed her hair away from her sweaty face. I was trying to remain calm, but panic welled up to suffocate me. *She has to snap out of this eventually, right? She's strong. There won't be any permanent mental damage. Please, Sam. Snap the fuck out of it. Please.*

I pressed in along the block in her mind again, trying to force my way through without doing any damage. Nothing happened. "Fucking shit!" I spat.

It was almost as if she was actively keeping me out of her mind, which made absolutely no sense. I'd just have to keep trying until either she fixed herself or I was finally able to break through.

"It's going to be okay. If you can hear me, it's going to be okay. You'll be okay." *I'll make sure of it, no matter the cost.*

Chapter 40

SAM

"You've got to be fucking kidding me."

I met the disdainful gaze of none other than myself, or rather my second personality I'd come to know as Samantha. Glancing wildly around, I remembered the sensation of the taint overflowing within me. I shuddered in revulsion. "What happened and why am I here talking to you again?"

"It's going to be okay. If you can hear me, it's going to be okay. You're going to be okay." Austin's voice wafted through the air as if being piped in on speakers.

Samantha grimaced. "Yeah, how about *you've* got to be fucking kidding *me*. I thought we had this all worked out. You gave me your permission to take control, and I was doing a pretty bang-up job of running things if you ask me. Austin and I were on the right track. I could feel it. And then ... I mean, suddenly you yanked the reins from me and have a first-class freak out. You nearly got us all killed. I mean, did you pick the exact worst moment to have your little breakdown? And where the hell did that—"

"I don't fucking know!" I screeched. "I don't know what the fuck happened."

Samantha paced back and forth in front of me, her mouth set in an angry line. She huffed out a sigh before snagging my gaze again. "I know what went wrong. It's the whole us intermingling thing. It worked much better when I could lock you away. I just kept all of the parts you couldn't handle a secret. Apparently, your conscience couldn't handle—"

"Life is precious! I don't want to live like you've been doing it. Joanna was a person and you acted like she didn't even matter." Sucking in a deep breath, I attempted to calm myself. It was definitely an effort in futility.

"Look at me, Chloe, and listen closely. You need me to get you out of this whole fucked-up situation. I'm not saying you're weak—" She scrunched up her nose and winced. "Okay, so maybe I am. But really, you're just the weak parts of our personality. If Natalie hadn't fucked with us, we'd balance each other out and be like a complete person. You, Chloe, are all of our soft squishy parts, and I'm all of the not-so-nice parts. The only thing we have in common is that we want the same things or the same outcomes. How we would get there ... totally different. Of course, that's assuming we'd get there with you in charge at all."

I opened my mouth to retort, but Samantha cut me off.

"I'm forcing the issue now. I'm done asking for permission. I'm done with all this bullshit. You need me ... we need me to be in charge if we have any hope of surviving this."

"I thought you said that you needed—"

Her fist slammed into the side of my face, and all went dark.

JOLTING AWAKE, I was instantly aware of who I was and what I needed to do.

I'm Samantha. And I have to keep Chloe locked away like I used to.

She couldn't handle the things I'd done or the things I was planning to do. I was fully aware that we were technically the same person, even if I didn't think of myself that way anymore. And I did eventually want us to merge—to be happy ... normal. I wasn't meant for the everyday world. I toed the line of a sociopath without Chloe. The only thing that kept me from going over that edge was my love for Austin. I was pretty sure a true sociopath didn't give two shits about anyone but themselves. I would die for Austin without the slightest bit of hesitation, although I'd rather not die at all. So perhaps I wasn't in danger of becoming a sociopath, just an everyday run-of-the-mill psycho.

When my eyes finally focused, they latched onto the

azure gaze of the man I loved, the reason all parts of me did anything.

A gloriously dazzling smile broke across his face, and he pulled me tightly into his arms. "I knew you'd snap out of it. I fucking knew it." His hands stroked down my back, trembling slightly. "You need to tell me what happened back there," he commanded roughly, even as his lips skimmed gently over my jawline.

"It doesn't matter. All you need to know is that everything is fine now."

Austin pulled away from me so his darkening gaze could peer into my face. He studied me for a moment before understanding flashed somewhere deep within his limpid pools. "Okay."

I idly wondered if he was having the same kind of battle with Alex as I'd had with Chloe. Or maybe Austin instinctively knew that it was me, Samantha, again. Or the most likely scenario … I was just completely batshit insane.

I dug my fingers into his shoulders. "We need to get back to that house and take care of Carlos."

"Agreed."

IT FELT a bit suicidal and stupid to head right back to the place where we'd almost been gunned down. Although the second time around we were going to be coming at the problem from a different angle. Not only would we be ready with weapons of our own, besides our abilities that is, but we also wouldn't be knocking on the front door again.

Tense and crouched along the side of the house, Austin and I both reached out to feel for Carlos with our minds. Realization slammed into me as Austin sucked in a startled intake of breath. Our gun-happy Carlos was already dead. The discovery was eerily similar to the situation in Pittsburgh when Nixon and I arrived to two recently deceased empaths.

Straightening myself up, I made my way to the front door and entered the house, knowing Austin wouldn't be far behind. Just inside of the foyer was Carlos. I immediately reached in, probing deep, to see if I could garner any useful information from him.

"Those fuckers aren't going to take me alive." Carlos focused on reloading his gun. He didn't hear someone approaching him from the kitchen until it was too late. Sudden pain ripped across his lower back, and then more of the same over and over again, causing him to drop to the ground. Just before he collapsed, he managed to get a good look at his attacker's face.

I ground my teeth together as I focused back in on the present. "Nixon."

Austin shook his head and tugged at his hair with agitation. "Why he might have killed Carlos could make sense if he's still working for Natalie, but how did he—"

"Wipe the emotions from the body without tampering with the memory? The memory is there because of the intense emotions, right? At least that's what I always thought. The only one who could ever alter that type of thing used to be Malcolm." I was as frustrated as Austin about the entire situation. Joanna had been warned, thus stealing the joy of her death from us. And now Carlos' body had been wiped of all emotions, leaving behind just the actual memory of his murder. Again, there was nothing for us to enjoy.

"What game is he playing? And how the fuck is he doing it?" Austin grated.

"Damned if I know. But we need to get the hell out of here. We'll just move on to the next person on the list. There's no point in crying over Carlos' spilled blood. We were going to kill him after we interrogated him anyways. And since we got nothing from Joanna as well—we're no worse off at least, even though I was hoping we'd have more answers by now."

"You're right, it's just ..." His voice trailed off and I met his gaze. He didn't want to say it, but he didn't have to since it was scrawled across his face within every tense line. He was jonesing for death emotions. His addiction, so much worse than mine, was starting to make him edgy.

And because I was Samantha and not Chloe, it didn't bother me in the least. I just wanted to ease Austin's pain.

I'll do anything for you.

I stepped into him, wrapping my hand around the back of his neck, and tilted his face down so our foreheads were touching. "Do you need to find someone else to take the edge off? I'm sure we can find someone nearby."

Austin's nostrils flared, his eyes widening. He hadn't

expected that reaction from me. "I— No. I think I can make it."

"Don't try to be strong on my account." I ran my hand up through the back of his hair and he shivered. "I love you, no matter what."

"I love you, too," he rasped just before leaning in to snag my lips. A deep, guttural groan sounded in the back of his throat when I deepened the kiss.

I broke away from him, laughing softly as he scrambled after me with his eyes still closed. "We need to get out of here. We'll finish what we started after we visit the next person on the list." Not only that but we would ride out the death emotions together. That idea had me chomping at the bit, too.

"How am I supposed to drive, or concentrate, or anything with this?" Austin rubbed his palm over the front of his jeans, showcasing his hard cock, which I was already aware of.

I quirked an eyebrow. "Oh, that? Let me take care of it for you."

I dropped to my knees in front of him, ignoring the fact that Carlos' dead body was almost too close for comfort. I shoved at Austin so his back hit the wall, and then I unzipped his pants. I sucked him directly into the back of my throat. There was no time for licking and teasing to draw things out. My goal was to make him come as quickly as possible, not that he would mind. I'm pretty sure that drawing it out was always more for my pleasure.

A few minutes later, Austin pulsed into my mouth, spurting hot liquid down the back of my throat. "Fuuuck," he ground out, his head thrown back, his muscles bunched in pleasure.

When I had swallowed down every last drop, I tucked him neatly back into his pants and zipped him up. I gazed up the line of his body, and he threaded his hands into my hair, his fingers gently kneading my scalp.

"Feel better?" I asked.

A slow grin spread across his face. "Much."

"Good, now let's go."

Chapter 41
SAM

I was asleep in my hotel room when I heard it ... the explosion that shook the walls. I scrambled from bed, instantly alert, my heart thrumming a rapid staccato inside my chest. The lights flickered briefly before another loud boom caused things to rattle more than the first time. I glanced at the little plastic-covered emergency exit map on the back of the door. I knew it was time to get the hell out of the hotel before it fell down around my ears. Scrambling around, I gathered my most important possessions—purse, laptop, jewelry, before throwing on some clothes and dashing for the door.

Outside in the hallway, other people hurried to vacate the premises; some cried, and some screamed in panic. A hotel employee sprinted down the hall, calling out for everyone to follow him but to not panic, everything would be fine. I gritted my teeth and fell in line with the other people trailing along behind him. Just then the floor shook, followed by another loud booming sound, and fire swished down the hallway, engulfing everyone in its path.

A moment before it overtook me, I turned to see the man behind me as he smiled and muttered, "Fifteen."

I screamed.

"Holy fuck!" I twisted out of Austin's grip, nearly banging my head on the steering wheel. "Not another one of those senseless fifteen dreams."

"They have to mean something or you wouldn't keep having them," Austin stated, keeping his eyes on the road.

"Well then, you tell me what you think it means. Fifteen, fifteen, fifteen." I punched the door and immediately regretted it as my hand began to throb.

"I don't know. I've been wracking my brain, but I haven't the faintest clue."

"The only thing in common with any of the scenarios is that they are all some kind of tragedy. An accident, a mass shooting … that and someone saying the number fifteen right before I wake up. It feels almost like someone is sending me a message. A very convoluted, dark message, but I can't shake the feeling that it's important to figure out."

A niggling feeling in my gut was telling me that not only was it important to figure out, but I needed to soon. There was a kind of desperation that clung to everything when I thought about it. I decided, just like I always did with situations such as those, to push it aside. "Who's the next person on the list?"

Austin jerked his head to the right. "Have a look for yourself."

I rolled my eyes, slumping back against the seat. "It doesn't really matter. I guess I'll find out when we get there." Sudden exhaustion threatened to pull me back under.

"Too lazy to reach into the glove compartment?" Austin chuckled.

A smile curled my lips up at the corners. I reached my arms out and then let them fall back to my lap when I couldn't reach the glove compartment without moving. "It's too far away."

"Guess you'll just have to wait and see then. I know how you love surprises."

I hated surprises. I had to be one of the most impatient people on the planet. "Yeah, whatever."

"Someone's cranky."

I shot Austin a dirty look. "I'm just ready for all of this to be over."

"Yeah, me too."

We fell into silence, our minds swirling around all the crap we'd been through lately. Austin cleared his throat like he was about to say something but then didn't.

I tipped my head back and shut my eyes. "Do you think it's ever honestly going to end? Or will we just keep going in circles like we have most of our lives?"

"We're going to make it end, one way or another," Austin muttered, more to himself than me.

I swallowed, my anxiety ratcheting up. I just hoped

things would break the way we wanted. So many things could go wrong with our burn-it-to-the-ground plan. *So many things.*

"Hey." Austin took my hand, raised it to his lips, and pressed a soft kiss against my skin. "Snap out of it. We got this."

"We got this," I forced myself to agree.

Austin rolled us into a smooth stop and threw the SUV into park. "We're here."

Sitting up, I mentally prepared myself, hoping we didn't get shot at again. "I'm ready."

Austin and I exited the SUV cautiously and faced house number three, which of course had a bright red door. I swore under my breath. "Are you willing to admit the whole red door thing is creepy yet?"

A frown tugged at Austin's lips. "All right. Fine. It has now officially become creepy."

"As if it wasn't before," I muttered.

Chapter 42
NIXON

I arrived at Carlos' house after Sam and Austin were already gone. Carlos was dead, of course. First Joanna and then Carlos … the trail of bodies was quickly beginning to add up. Natalie had expressed her great displeasure when I'd called in for another clean-up team. She didn't like that Sam and Austin were off the grid, and that I wasn't directly following them anymore, but rather trying to second-guess their next move.

But when I felt them approach where I was waiting for them, I knew I'd finally played the right hand, and I was about to throw all my chips in the game. I'd already taken care of the empath that they were coming to see. He wasn't very powerful in comparison to Austin and Sam, but stealing his abilities gave mine a boost, and every little bit would help with what was to come.

Right off the bat, I noticed that Sam felt different … darker. It was almost as if she was missing a part of herself, or she'd walled it off like she used to do. And Austin, he was the same. The two of them were a fucked-up matched set. *Not for long. Austin's time on this planet is about to come to an end.*

Anticipation coursed through my system. Sam would be mine again soon, and this time for good.

But the knock on the front door didn't come.

Things went sideways in a way I could never have anticipated.

Chapter 43

SAM

Muscular arms wrapped around my middle, yanking me away from Austin. Neither one of us saw or heard him approach. Austin's surprise intermingled with mine just before Nixon's void shield dropped down to isolate me from him and my own abilities.

"Let me go!" I screamed, thrashing within his grasp.

"She doesn't want you," Austin grated. "When are you going to get that through your thick skull?"

"It doesn't matter." Nixon laughed. "She doesn't need to want me."

I met Austin's gaze, his expression of confusion mirroring mine. Something didn't seem quite right about Nixon, but before I put my finger on it, a second Nixon shoved through the front door of the house, brandishing a 9mm handgun pointed in our direction.

"Let her go. I don't care who you are, I'll shoot first

and ask questions later."

Austin's head swung around when the second Nixon spoke. It hit me then that the real Nixon had been telling us the truth all along and that someone actually was pretending to be him. But why?

"What if you miss and shoot her instead?" Faux Nixon sneered.

"I'm a damn good shot," Nixon snapped. "I won't miss."

"No one is infallible. Are you willing to risk her life?"

I stopped fighting Faux Nixon so the real Nixon had a better chance of his shot hitting its target. "That won't help," Faux Nixon stage whispered. "Think about it. If I have the power to look like him, then I have the power to shift our images to make sure he misses."

Nixon stopped dead in his tracks, and Austin swore.

"Ahh, I see now you've all realized what you're dealing with."

"What do you want from us?" I rasped.

"From all of you? Nothing. From you? Everything." He shifted, ramming a needle into my neck.

The last thing I heard were Austin and Nixon's angry bellows.

"DID YOU MISS ME?" Malcolm's familiar voice mocked.

My face slackened as I repeatedly blinked, trying to make the hallucination disappear. "No, you died. I saw you die. I *felt* you die."

"Obviously it was a lie."

My hand trembled as I brought it up to my mouth. I couldn't drag my gaze away from him. Malcolm looked exactly the same as I remembered him. His brown hair and innocent doe eyes, as deceptive as ever to anyone who couldn't sense the malice in him. "No, you're dead. This is a nightmare. A horrible, horrible realistic nightmare."

"So sorry to disappoint, but it's not. I am very real and very much alive." He grinned at me. "God, I've been waiting for this moment for so long. It took so much planning and so much effort. So many things nearly went wrong, and now it's finally coming together just the way I want."

My mind flashed back to another time.

"THIS MIGHT HURT A BIT," *Malcolm murmured, his amusement evident.*

His forced presence in my mind was an assault on all my senses, bogging me down and pulling me under into a lake of tar, the thick substance consuming me completely.

Screaming, I tried to eject him, but he was too strong—stronger than I thought—and I couldn't beat him, not like I thought I could. If only I'd listened to—

"I'M STRONGER NOW. Even the last time we were together I'm sure you realized that. And that was just—"

"I am, too." Malcolm sneered. "Plus, I have new

abilities to play with. As I'm sure you've realized." Right before my eyes, his appearance morphed into Nixon again.

I narrowed my eyes, searching for a flaw in the deception but spotting none. "You can do what Cal did."

"Yesss," he purred. "It's because I stole his ability from him. Did it right in front of Austin and he didn't realize it. The two of you have been so easy to play. You're blind to everything but each other."

My mind was reeling as it skittered back through so many events that I couldn't make sense of. But now …

"You. It's been you this whole time, hasn't it? Everything … But why? Why do you hate Austin so much?" I didn't know why I bothered asking. I already knew the answer. It was because of Maggie.

"Yes, it's all because of Maggie. It's always been because of her. Remember when I said the fun was just beginning?"

He shoved a memory at me, forcing me to relive it.

"Time to get up and play." Malcolm's hot breath fanned across my cheek.

I jerked into motion, trying to scramble away from him, but my hands were bound behind my back, something I'd temporarily forgotten. I surveyed the small room I was being held in, realizing I didn't have anywhere to go. My world suddenly tilted.

"Aw … I think you got up too fast," Malcolm said with mock concern. "You might want to take it slow."

"Fuck you," I grated.

"That's not very nice, Chloe. I'm just trying to help." He regarded me with doe-like brown eyes that would have been beautiful if there was anything but darkness behind them.

"My name hasn't been Chloe for a long time, it's—"

"Sam. I know, I know. I do suppose if we're going to be working together I really should start calling you by your new name, huh?"

"I'll never work with you," I spat.

"Now, now, Sam. Hasn't anyone ever told you to never say never?"

"I'm not going to work with you—ever. And you won't take me from Austin—ever. We share a special connection. The only way you can break that is by killing me, and from what I just heard, that isn't going to happen. So sorry."

Ignoring me, he tapped his chin. "Now where to begin?"

"Who the hell are you working for anyways? Who would employ a psycho like you?" I mean really, what kind of place would keep a complete sociopath with so much power on the payroll?

A smile ghosted across Malcolm's lips. "The United States Government, of course."

My eyes widened. "Wh-What?" I stammered. "But I thought—"

"Oh, you thought that's who ran your little operation, didn't you? I'm afraid not. Our ex-employer is privately funded by some do-gooder who has more money on their hands than they know what to do with. Kind of a waste if you ask me. But my employer, and your soon-to-be new employer, focuses on political manipulation. I don't think I need to expound on that

any further. At your old place of employment, you might have gotten to save some lives, but here? Here you'll get to shape history."

"I'm not interested in shaping history, unless it entails saving lives."

Malcolm rolled his eyes. "I don't have the patience for your sanctimonious, holier-than-thou drivel right now. I want to get started on tinkering with that mind of yours. Or maybe first we should take a trip down memory lane ... again."

My stomach somersaulted, and I was swept into a memory. But instead of playing out slowly, it slammed into me, only pieces of it standing out in my mind.

"Oh, Austin—yes, Austin!"

"I'm sorry, Malcolm. So sorry. More than you'll ever know. But it had to be done. You have to know it had to be done."

"Why? Why would you do this to me?"

"You know why."

"I love her! You know I love her! How could you do this to me?"

"You screwed up. You fell in too deep. You'll get over it and realize what you felt wasn't really love. She had to die. You know she had to die."

"No! I love her! Maggie. Please. I love you. Maggie ... I need her. Please, I need her."

"No! Stop! You're not going to turn me against him!" My chest heaved as I sucked in ragged breaths. "Nothing you can show me will ever turn me against him."

Malcolm was on me in a second, his fingers digging into my throat, his lips pulled back from his teeth in a snarl, spittle flying from his mouth. "You will see. I'll make you see."

His inky mind slithered into mine, contaminating everything it touched. "No!" I screamed, thrashing against him.

Images of Austin with a myriad of women swam in front of my mind's eye—him kissing them, him touching them, him fucking them. It was one thing to know he'd been with a lot of women, but it was something entirely different to see it. And there was no point in trying to deny the truth of it because I knew that Malcolm had gotten the information I was currently viewing directly from Austin's mind.

Malcolm kept bombarding me with unwanted images of Austin and other women until they choked me, and I gagged on bile. "Stop. Please stop." I curled into a ball, my hands still bound behind my back. "It doesn't matter. I still love him. I still love him," I whispered, trying to comfort myself.

The images cut off just as suddenly as they began. "Then you're a bigger fool than I thought," Malcolm spat. "And the fun is just beginning."

I WAS WELCOMED back to the present by a soft sniggering from Malcolm. "Everyone thought I was just going to play their game. Everyone thought I just rolled over and died so easily. This," he flicked his hand between me and him, "is how it ends for you. It's been my plan since the very beginning."

"You sound like a villain in a badly scripted movie," I scoffed, trying to push down my fear.

"As you've said before." He rolled his eyes. "At least come up with something new."

"Are you going to finally give me the villain run down of everything you've done? I think after everything you've put me through you owe me that much."

Malcolm dragged an aluminum chair from a desk and set it a few feet from me. He spun it around and straddled it, resting his chin on his forearms in a lazy manner. It was then that I finally scanned my new surroundings. Nothing special, just the standard run-of-the-mill holding space that I'd sadly become so accustomed to … bland colors, and only large enough for a bed and a desk.

"Well?" I persisted.

"I'm talking to Samantha, aren't I? I've always liked you better than Chloe." Malcolm smiled at me, a knowing glint in his eyes.

I should have been surprised, but somehow I wasn't. "Well, aren't you just a big fucking know it all?" Curiosity overwhelmed me though. I wanted the answers I was now sure Malcolm held.

Malcolm rocked back in his chair, rolling his eyes. "All right … fine. I wouldn't want you to die disappointed."

I sat forward on the bed, staring at him expectantly. My fear had temporarily taken a backburner, overridden by my thirst for answers. Plus, hopefully, I could draw out Malcolm's little confession, since he did seem to like the sound of his own voice, and by that time Austin, as well as Nixon, would ride to the rescue. Two birds, one stone, and all that jazz.

Chapter 44
MALCOLM

Sam thought she was so smart. Her, Austin, and Nixon all did. But I'd patronize her with my story, let her think I was falling for her stall tactic. After all, I'd been itching to tell the details to someone so she would have to do. Too bad, in the end, my effort would be wasted since she'd be dead soon.

I tapped my chin, giving her a tight-lipped smile. "I suppose I'll start with the part of the tale you know. The part where Austin stole Maggie from me. You already know how I trusted him, how he was like a brother to me —" I stopped short, my anger threatening to overwhelm me. I focused on my plans for Sam, letting the image of her body lying cold and lifeless in front of me settle a calm into my bones.

I inhaled deeply several times. "Yes, so, he stole the love of my life, my other half." My voice rose in anger again. "My fucking soul."

Trembling, I forced myself to continue in a steady tone. "And just when I thought I'd get to do the same to him in return, I was ordered not to. You remember, I just showed you that memory."

Her nostrils flared and she nodded almost imperceptibly but stayed quiet.

"They wanted him. They already had me. Again, I wasn't good enough. Keep you alive to make him happy—what about me?" I slammed my fists against the top of the chair, and she flinched.

Grinding my teeth together, I again let myself conjure the outcome of my plans, which would finally bring justice. *You're finally going to make Austin pay. For you, Maggie. It's all for you.* "I know you're aware of Project Reaper and you now remember your childhood and how you first met Austin. I also know that you've come to terms with the division of Samantha and Chloe, and Alex and Austin … all part of the process. But what you still don't know will stagger you."

"Would you just spit it out already?" Samantha tried to feign indifference, but I knew better. She wanted the answers desperately. Not that I could really blame her.

I tapped my fingers rapidly across the edge of the chair. "David and Natalie were so committed to the program that they admitted their own children to it." That got a reaction out of her. Her eyes widened and she rocked backwards with surprise.

I grinned. "Me and …" I watched her closely, waiting to drop the bomb. "Nixon." Her jaw went slack, which caused me to chuckle. "He doesn't even know we're brothers. But I do." I waved my hand in the air, not wanting to talk about Nixon. He was irrelevant. "That's neither here nor there for the time being." I shifted on the chair. "As cruel as it was to experiment on their own children, Natalie and David did have a soft spot for the two of us. They—"

"That's why you weren't killed, and that's why Nixon was left in charge ... and why—"

"Yes, to all of it. Makes perfect sense now, doesn't it?" I gave her a smug smile. Her and Austin thought they were on the right track, thought they were going to figure everything out on their own. They didn't have a fucking clue.

"Is Nixon ... is Nixon two personalities? Are you?" she croaked.

"Yes. But dear ole' mom did another thing to Nixon. She tried to force the two of you to bond so she could remove Austin from the equation." I rolled my eyes at the absurdity of it. "Obviously it didn't work, at least not on your end. She merely created an obsession on his part. She's in denial of course. She's such a great mother," I spat.

I hated Natalie. She'd been the one to order Maggie's death, using Austin to carry out the sentence and making him into something I hated almost as much as her. Natalie had made Maggie the way she was ... she'd made us all the way that we were, and then suddenly she couldn't handle the way things turned out. She hadn't wanted me to turn out like Austin, but I had. She thought killing Maggie would fix the problem. And Austin just went and did it like a good little boy. He should have protected me—protected the woman I loved. Not fucked and then killed her.

Rage burned through my veins, and I stood suddenly, throwing the chair against the wall. I yanked at my hair, attempting to center myself. None of that mattered anymore. I'd finally managed to make Sam like Maggie, and Austin had been affected I had been. They were exactly like us, and I was going to do to Austin what he'd done to me. Then I'd make Natalie pay. They would all pay. I just had to stay focused.

Exhaustion overwhelmed me, and the little game I'd been playing with Sam, revealing tidbits of information, all seemed pointless. "I'm done with this conversation," I growled, stalking to the door.

"Wait!" Sam exclaimed.

"No. I'll be back later."

Chapter 45

SAM

Slumping onto the bed after Malcolm left, my mind reeled with uncertainty as it attempted to fit the pieces of the puzzle he'd revealed together. Malcolm and Nixon brothers? The both of them Natalie and David's children? Hell, the fact that Malcolm was still alive was enough of a shock.

They say hindsight is 20/20, and as I looked back at the events since Maggie was killed, I'd have to agree. And, Nixon, knowing that his obsession with me wasn't entirely his fault … well, that put a whole new spin on things, too. Austin and I had read about it in his chart, but somehow it didn't seem real until Malcolm confirmed it.

So what happens now?

A memory flashed into my mind, completely unbidden, as if to answer my question.

"Join me, won't you, Sam?" Malcolm's voice purred in my

mind. I knew what he wanted: For me to slide with him into his current victim's mind as they died. And it wasn't a request.

"No."

"As if you have a choice."

And he was right, twofold. If I didn't do exactly what he demanded, I was risking Austin's safety in the long run, but Malcolm also knew how much I craved what he was offering me. My grand plan with him—all of it—I had to wonder if a part of me was merely using Malcolm as an excuse to feel the deaths I didn't want to admit I yearned for. At any rate, resistance was futile, and we both knew it.

Regardless, I tried to resist. Staring myself down in the tiny mirror, I gripped the sink so tightly my knuckles turned white. Sweat gathered along my hairline and upper lip.

Malcolm's mind tugged on mine, and I gritted my teeth. "No," I croaked. "Not this time."

Malcolm's taunting laugh ricocheted inside my skull. "Every time, Sam, every time."

And with that, I was no longer aware of my body's surroundings because I was seeing out of someone else's eyes.

Dirty fucking bastards double-crossed me. I should have known. I should have been more cautious. Shoulda, coulda, woulda ... didn't. Fuck. My father always said my ambition and lack of scruples would be the end of me one day. Fucking old coot, guess he was right. What the hell is this sick fuck waiting for? Why doesn't he finish the job instead of leaving me here paralyzed? I can't move a damn muscle. We both know he's going to kill me, so why doesn't he just get it the fuck over with?

"Ready, Sam? This one is going to be a fast high."

Shit, that's a big gun. I hope this doesn't hurt too much. Fuck, why doesn't he just do it already? Why the fu—

The click of the hammer was the only distinguishable sound before everything exploded in a wash of red. I squeezed my eyes shut as I became aware of my own body again. Goose bumps erupted across my skin, and my breaths were quick and shallow like I had just sprinted up a few flights of stairs. The familiar euphoria pumped through my system, leaving me floating in its bliss. The death that both Malcolm and I had just experienced was a shock to my system. The suddenness of it so powerful, so—

Feverish lips crashed into mine as a large, solid body lifted me and pushed tightly against me. Instinctively, I wrapped my legs around that body, not even bothering to open my eyes, grinding myself against the source of my newfound pleasure. The death's euphoria only served to heighten all of my senses, and my nerve endings danced with anticipation of what would happen next.

Austin's image danced through my mind, his piercing azure gaze filled with love and devotion as he stared down at me.

My eyes flew open, and I registered Malcolm's pale face so close it was a blur. Bile climbed into my throat as I wrenched myself abruptly away, shoving at his chest. "What the hell do you think you're doing?"

Blinking his doe-like eyes, he slid reluctantly away from me. "I-I—" he stammered before regaining his composure. "I needed to share the aftereffects with someone, and you're as good as anyone." He shrugged before donning a signature smirk.

Shuddering with revulsion, I wiped my lips with the back of my hand demonstratively. "You mean like you used to with Maggie?" I bared my teeth at him. "So sorry. Just like her, I'd rather have Austin."

Anguish followed by anger flashed in Malcolm's dark eyes. Before I had time to move, the back of his hand cracked into the side of my face. My head whipped to the left, and I hit the other side of my face against the wall. The sharp metallic tang of my blood bloomed in my mouth.

"Don't ever speak of what Maggie and I had together. You could never begin to understand."

Turning to look at him, I ran my tongue along the inside of my cheek "Oh, I'm more than beginning to understand."

Glaring at him defiantly, I dared him to hit me again because this time I was ready. But he just stood there, staring at me with hatred rolling off of him in palpable waves, despite me having a lock on my shields.

"She probably never really loved you, and I'm guessing you never really loved her. What just happened between us proves it. I hate you, and I'm pretty sure you hate me, and yet—" I shuddered in revulsion again. "We were just ..." I couldn't bring myself to say it out loud.

AS IT TURNED OUT, I really didn't understand what was between Malcolm and Maggie. Not at all. I now believed that Malcolm had loved Maggie at least. I still wasn't convinced of her love for him though. And for the first time, what happened between Malcolm and me in that bathroom took on a darker connotation. He was intent on revenge. He wanted me to be like Maggie, and Austin to suffer like he did.

I gasped. How could I have been so stupid? How could I have missed something so fucking obvious? He wanted to seduce me away from Austin, or at least to fuck me, and then he wanted to kill me. Kissing me had been the first step. Perhaps he was lonely, and maybe the only way for him to touch me was after a kill when we were both riding the death emotions. Everything else that happened between then and now …

Malcolm had been drawing it out. It would make the revenge so much sweeter for him. Austin and I going around and around in circles, giving us—or really, giving Austin—false hope that we would be together, only to yank it away at the last minute. All of it was meant to make it worse for Austin.

I also finally understood that none of it was about me. It was all about Austin for Malcolm. I was positive that Malcolm was the darker half of his personality, just like Samantha and Austin were for Chloe and Alex. Austin would have been the same way if I had been killed. Was that also part of the plan? Was Malcolm still going to deliver Austin over to Project Reaper on a silver platter after he killed me? Or was he planning to kill Austin, too?

Rolling onto my stomach, I pressed my face into my forearm and screamed in frustration. Everything was Natalie and David's fault, and whoever else was behind Project Reaper. How could I have been fooled so completely by Natalie? Why did she try to bond Nixon with me when I was already linked to Austin? The questions that I now had weren't as significant as before though. Malcolm, even though he'd gotten angry and left, had answered so much for me, even if I'd been the one to read between the lines of the information he provided.

What mattered now was making sure that Malcolm didn't finally accomplish what he'd set out to do with his plan for revenge. I used to be cocky when it came to him, but I'd learned my lesson. He was the puppet master behind everything. He actually was like some movie villain, even the part where he'd made us all believe he was dead.

Then, just when we could see the light at the end of the tunnel, *BAM* he showed up out of nowhere. I was left with a level of paranoia that I'd surprisingly never experienced before. Was Malcolm really the driving force behind everything? Or because I kept thinking of him like a movie villain, specifically one from the '80s, was I just painting him that way in my mind? There was no real way of knowing.

Austin and Nixon would come for me, that much I did know. I just hoped Malcolm's plans weren't as well thought out as he made them seem. Although, for him to have gotten as far as he did with everything, I was afraid... terrified even, and that was usually Chloe's territory.

Chapter 46
AUSTIN

"I should have shot him. I could have done it. I should have … I—"

I tuned out Nixon who was blubbering on and on about not being able to stop the other Nixon from taking Sam. He was having a fucking breakdown. I, on the other hand, knew that allowing my emotions to rule me in this instance would do no one any good … especially Sam. I needed to stay cool and focused so I would see her in one piece again.

My mind rifled through what I knew, which wasn't much. Someone was pretending to be Nixon. I was assuming he had an ability like Cal's. He wanted Sam … for what? Why was everyone always trying to rip her away from me? She really had been better off without me in her life. If only she hadn't been so stubborn, if only I hadn't been so weak.

"Fuuuuuuck." I marched over to Nixon and

backhanded him across the face. His head whipped to the side, and he stilled, his breathing ragged. "You need to snap the fuck out of it. She's gone. The question is—are you going to continue to blubber like a little bitch, or are you going to help me get her back?"

Nixon turned towards me, his eyes blazing with hatred. "If you would have just stayed away from her—"

"Yeah, yeah, yeah. How many times am I going to have to hear that one? Again … you can't go back and change it. What is … *is*."

Nixon's right eye twitched, his expression suddenly calm. "So we stop trying to kill each other until Sam is safe?"

I knew he wanted me dead, but actively trying to kill me was an entirely different story. I had my suspicions, but now they were confirmed. *Huh. Good to know*. "Yep. And as soon as she's safe, and she's back in *my* arms … we can go back to trying to kill each other." *Of course I'll be the winner, as usual, when it came down to the two of us.*

"I'll let you kiss her goodbye before I kill you. How about that?" Nixon grated, his lips twisting up into a demented grin.

I laughed. "I knew you were delusional but that's taking it to a whole new level." I moved towards the SUV and pulled the keys from my pocket. "I'm driving."

"Do you have any idea where we're going?"

"Nope, but I'm thinking we should get out of here first, and then we can figure it out."

"Just like Sam."

I smirked. "That's why the two of us are so good together."

"No, that's why the two of you are bad together. You're too much alike."

I didn't bother dignifying him with an answer. Sam and I were a perfect fit for each other. We always had been and always would be. Nothing could change that. Especially not a twisted, fucked in the head ex-best friend like Nixon.

Once we were in the car and heading out of the residential neighborhood, Nixon cleared his throat to get my attention. "I suppose there are a few things I need to tell you."

I glanced over at him and quirked an eyebrow.

"Natalie wants you dead now, too. In fact, she sent me to kill you. My reward is Sam. I was going to be permitted to take her and disappear for good."

I threw my head back and laughed before returning my gaze to the road. "And you believed her? After you did her dirty work for her, she'd either have the two of you killed or—"

"She's my mother," he blurted out, completely stunning me. The other Nixon, the false one, had told me that, but I'd thought it was a lie. Hearing the real Nixon say it made it concrete, and I was shocked more than the first time I'd heard it.

"The other Nixon knew that, too. Whoever he is knows a hell of a lot about all of us. And why after all this time does Natalie want me dead?"

Nixon shrugged. "Don't know and don't care. It fit with my plans, so I didn't bother asking."

I grunted. Of course, he wanted to believe her. He thought he was going to get Sam. "Something is off about the whole thing."

"Like I said, I don't care."

He should care. It didn't really matter to me either though. It just would have been nice to know what I was working with. "How do we find her?"

"I have a feeling whoever took her is going to make his presence known. We should find a place to lay low and wait for him to contact us."

"What makes you think—"

"He wanted her alive. It's why I should have shot him. He was bluffing. The only reason he might want her alive is if he wants something from one or both of us."

It made sense. "And whoever it is spent all this time fucking with us … playing a game with us. He wouldn't just end it like that so easily. Any idea who it could be? I didn't see anyone in those files who had an ability like Cal's. He was the only one, and obviously he's dead."

"No. Cal was the only one I knew of, and if there's nothing in those files …"

We fell into silence. I couldn't shake the eerie feeling that the only person I could think of who seemed to enjoy such over-the-top dramatics was … Malcolm. But he was dead. So we were dealing with someone completely unknown. *Fucking great.*

Chapter 47
SAM

An eternity seemed to tick by as I waited for Malcolm to return. The nerves and anticipation curdled in my gut. I tried reaching out to Austin, knowing what the results would ultimately be.

My thoughts kept returning to Malcolm though. Was he keeping me waiting to up my anxiety levels or was he out there somewhere putting into motion more nefarious things? Either one was completely plausible.

I can't believe he's still alive. How is it even possible? I replayed the scene of his supposed death over and over in my mind.

"Brace yourself. Now," Austin's voice commanded in my mind.

With no time to contemplate how he'd gotten past my barriers, I braced myself against the dash in Malcolm's car. Glancing in the rearview mirror, I spotted a black pickup truck barreling down on us. Knowing what was about to happen, I unsnapped Malcolm's seat belt before bracing myself fully again.

Malcolm's gaze darted between me and the road. "What are you—"

The truck smashed into the back of the car, shoving us forward while Malcolm struggled to keep us on the road. The truck revved, and tires squealed, as we were pushed towards the line of trees off to the right of us. Reflexively I screamed, the sound of grinding metal filling the air.

What the fuck is Austin thinking? Sure this might kill Malcolm, but it could kill me, too.

"Trust me," Austin rumbled low in my mind.

Adrenaline pumped through my system as the car lurched forward in a sudden motion. Malcolm sailed through the windshield as we rammed into one of the trees. With a pop and a hiss, the car came to an abrupt stop, the sudden lack of motion jarring. I watched numbly as Malcolm dragged himself to his feet and staggered towards the trees. A loud shot rang out, and he crumpled to the ground in a heap.

I didn't even hesitate to slip into his mind.

This isn't the way it's supposed to happen. She promised me I would win. She promised me I could make Austin pay by using Sam. This isn't the way it's supposed to happen. Why would she lie? Why would she—

Gasping, I snapped back into my own mind, the now familiar feeling of euphoria surging through my system. It was made that much better with the knowledge that it was Malcolm's death I'd just experienced.

He's dead. He's finally fucking dead.

Although after everything he'd put me and everyone I loved through, it was anticlimactic, too easy.

I'D BEEN RIGHT. It had been too easy. All of it.

But wait. I felt his death emotions—I felt them as he died. How could both of those things be true? How could Malcolm be alive and yet I'd been in his mind when he died? *I'm in denial. That has to be the answer. I don't want to admit to myself that I accepted his false death so easily.*

No. I saw him. I fucking saw him die. Felt him die. Death emotions couldn't be faked, and yet somehow Malcolm had managed it. "No, goddamnit! He was dead. He was fucking dead." I tugged at my hair in frustration. There had to be some other explanation. There just had to be.

"Occam's Razor," I mumbled. Maybe it was that simple … he'd been dead. Nothing was faked. *Yes, that has to be it.* He'd died but had been resuscitated. I hadn't considered the possibility that anyone would actually want to do such a thing. Obviously, I'd been mistaken.

I huffed out a breath and settled back down on the bed. I felt a tad better—a bit saner knowing that Malcolm had actually died and had simply been brought back. He couldn't fake death emotions. No one could. Two things in life were certain: death and taxes. At least I thought that's the way the saying went.

The door swung open, hitting the wall with a startling thud, but instead of Malcolm like I'd been expecting,

Austin stood not more than a few feet away from me. Squealing with joy, I rushed him, throwing myself into his arms.

"Sammy, my Sammy girl," he husked. "Don't worry. He's dead. Malcolm's dead for real this time. I made sure of it. No one will save him this time."

I plunged my tongue into his mouth with fervor. "I need you, Austin. Oh God, I fucking need you." I peppered his face and jawline with kisses.

His mind was closed off to me when I tried to slip in, but I didn't find it odd under the circumstances. Then again … Wouldn't he be riding the high from Malcolm's death emotions? Wouldn't he want to share them with me? Of course he would. Doubt prickled along my senses. Unless … Unless it was a less-than-satisfying kill. Although—

When Austin's hands slid down to cup my ass, all thoughts fled my mind.

He staggered to the bed, unceremoniously dropping me onto it. After shoving my pants down to my ankles, he spun me around. I gripped the bed as he climbed onto the mattress and plunged into me from behind. His fingers bit into my hips as he pounded in and out of my slick heat.

"Yes, Austin, oh yes!" I screamed, a sudden orgasm seizing my body.

"Fifteen," wafted across my mind. I shook my head, ignoring it.

Austin pulled out, ripped my pants off completely, and

flipped me over. "I want you to look at me, Sam. Look at me."

I lifted my gaze to his beautiful baby blues. They were churning with so many emotions. Angst, torment—but I wasn't sure why. The need to reassure him washed over me. "I love you," I murmured.

Austin's emotions blasted into me, filling up my entire head, spiking pain through my skull. Shock, pain, anguish … too much, it was all too much for me to process. And they were coming from—

My head rolled to the side, and my eyes widened as I took in the sight of Austin standing just inside of the open door, horror twisting his beautiful features.

What? I don't understand. How can he be there and—

A dark, maniacal laugh slammed into me, chilling me to my core. I whipped my head back to peer up at the Austin who was currently inside me. Blue eyes darkened to brown. Nearly black hair lightened to a mousy brown. A sharp jawline softened slightly …

No, no, no, no. He can't. It isn't. I would have known. How didn't I know? My limbs went numb, my body shutting down in an effort to not process what was happening.

Malcolm grinned down at me. "Surprise."

Time slowed to a crawl, every action and movement crystal clear, and yet I couldn't draw the power to alter what I knew was coming.

Malcolm grabbed my head, his fingers digging into my scalp, making it difficult for me to move. I dug my nails into his forearms, drawing blood, but Malcolm didn't even flinch, he merely dropped more of his body weight down on me so I had no leverage to fight him off as I thrashed beneath him.

"Oh wait, I almost forgot." Malcolm's features morphed again, this time into Nixon's. He turned to look at Austin, and then the real Nixon beside him. They both exploded into motion, panic on their faces.

But it was too late. I'd known that fact the moment I'd spotted Austin in the doorway.

I pushed all the knowledge I'd obtained from Malcolm at Austin in a jumble, hoping it would help him somehow.

Anguish and regret rolled through my system as I whispered into his mind, "*I love you.*"

And then, as if I had no control over my mouth, "Fifteen," fell from my lips, reverberating through my skull.

Malcolm twisted my head to the side sharply and a deafening crack blotted out my world.

Chapter 48

AUSTIN

I knew what I saw but my brain couldn't—wouldn't accept it. Sam, my Sam, my wife was writhing in ecstasy underneath someone who wasn't me but looked identical to me.

Rage and anguish twisted within my chest, strangling my heart.

Between one breath and the next, Malcolm loomed over my wife, his body entwined with hers.

This had been his end game all along.

He'd wanted me to not just feel the same level of pain as he had when he lost Maggie, but the exact same pain. Of course, I hadn't had to use complicated convolutions to spread Maggie's legs for me, but I was sure Malcolm was too far gone to see the difference. Didn't he know that I wouldn't blame Sam? Didn't he realize that I'd love her no matter—

His appearance morphed again to take on Nixon's appearance.

"She died in my arms. I saw her die in my arms." Nixon's words swam through my head, the ones he'd shared about his vision.

Nixon and I exploded into action, desperation thickening the air. We weren't fast enough, our movements bogged down as if we were stuck in molasses. I focused in on Malcolm as his hands moved to Sam's head, her expression calm.

A jumble of information was shoved into my mind, Sam sharing everything she could as quickly as she could manage. Images and thought fragments, emotions, and revelations about Malcolm, Nixon, and—

"I love you," Sam whispered in my mind.

No, no, no, no, no. It's not too late. Hold on. Don't give up. Just hold on. I'm right here. It's not going to end like this.

"Fifteen," slipped from her mouth just as Malcolm yanked her head to the side abruptly, a thunderous crack striking my ears.

Time slowed to a crawl as I continued towards Sam, my mind and body on autopilot, my eyes riveted to Sam's limp body. *No, no, no, no, no.*

Nixon reached the bed first, tearing Malcolm away from Sam. I dropped to my knees beside her, her gaze dull and lifeless. *No, no, no, no, no.*

"Sam, please." I reached a trembling hand up to touch her, my fingers skating over her already cooling flesh. I recoiled, not wanting to feel anymore, not wanting to remember her as anything but full of life and vibrant. "You can't leave me."

But she didn't respond, didn't so much as blink. Because she was dead.

He killed her. He killed my Sam. She's dead because of him.

My next breath lodged in my throat. *Sam, please. I can't go on without you. I can't. How can I possibly? Not again. I can't go on again without you.*

I somehow managed to tug her pants back on, needing to take care of her even in death. To give her some dignity when so much had been taken from her already. Then I swiped at her eyelids, hiding away her dull gaze—a gaze that would never register my presence again.

She'd left me behind, even if it wasn't voluntary. She'd gone somewhere I couldn't follow, couldn't get to her. After I got her back the last time, I didn't think there would ever be such a place. I didn't think—

Maybe there isn't. I could follow her. Why shouldn't I? What's the point of going on anymore? What's the point in anything without her? I did it before when I thought she was dead, and I barely survived. Or maybe on some level, I knew she wasn't really dead, and I'd merely been biding my time. Now I know. Now there's no doubt. Even when I'd tried to push her away for her own good, some part of me always knew it was useless. Her and I are one soul. Neither one of us could ever stay away from the other for too long.

What do you do when one-half of your soul is ripped away from you?

The bubble of silence around me and Sam slowly

dissipated, a steady rhythm of flesh against flesh meeting my ears, intermingled with laughter. Outrage beat within my veins, the notion of someone feeling anything but remorse in the presence of Sam's lifeless body insulting.

Lifting my head, I spotted Nixon on top of Malcolm, straddling his chest. Nixon gasped for breath, choking on his despair as he beat Malcolm's already bloody face to a pulp with nothing but his bare knuckles.

Malcolm continued to laugh, the sound wet and labored.

Malcolm's eyes flicked to me, and they gleamed with triumph. "Now you know. Now you finally know."

I pulled myself to my feet, my limbs numb. "And now you're going to know." I bared my teeth at him. "Now you're going to know what real pain feels like."

Nixon paused in his beating, his wild gaze meeting mine. We had a silent conversation, him and I. We would make Malcolm suffer. He would beg us for death by the end. Then and only then would we let him die.

Nixon yanked Malcolm to his feet, blood dripping from the both of them. "Where do you want him?"

Burning in hell. "Get a chair." My mind began conjuring up different modes of torture, none that I had actual experience with, but for Malcolm, Sam's killer, somehow I would figure it all out.

"WHAT DOES THE NUMBER FIFTEEN MEAN?" I shouted at the ruined flesh that used to be Malcolm's face.

Sam was dead, so I didn't know why I cared about any of it anymore, but the fact that she'd been having dreams with the number, and it was the last thing she said before Malcolm killed her, it had to mean something important. And I would find the answer for her. Focusing on getting that last scrap of information was the only thing currently keeping me sane.

But what was I hoping for, a way to bring her back to life? A way to rewind time so I could get a do-over? There was nothing Malcolm could tell me that would change the ending of our story. I'd lost my Sam ... I'd lost everything.

Darkness pooled in my middle, twisting and gathering. Not able to hold it back anymore, it exploded from me and barreled into Malcolm. He screamed in agony, the sound bringing a smile to my lips.

"Stop," Nixon hissed as he took hold of my shoulders. "We can't kill him yet. He might have information we can use."

"Use for what?" I seethed. "Nothing he can tell us will bring her back." My voice cracked. "She's gone."

"We have to make them pay," Nixon persisted, his fingers digging into my flesh. "We have to—" His words shriveled on his tongue as Malcolm slumped over in the chair he was tied to.

He's dead. The bastard is finally fucking dead.

But I needed to make sure this time.

"Let's burn his body." Not that it would make a difference in the end. If Malcolm miraculously survived like before, what else could he do to me? He'd ripped the one thing from my life that actually mattered. The gaping hole left in my chest by Sam was threatening to swallow me whole. I didn't want to live in a world without her—I couldn't.

"Wh-What about … her?" Nixon stumbled over the words. "Should we … should we—" He ran his hands through his hair and tugged with desperation. "This isn't real. It can't be. We're in some cell right now, or I am, and they're fucking with my head. They just want me to think she's dead. None of this is real. Or Malcolm gave her something to make us think she's dead. There are drugs, there are … it just isn't real." Nixon staggered, leaning into the wall to stay upright, a single tear sliding down his cheek.

I fucking wished more than anything that what he was saying was true. But I knew in my gut that she was dead. I felt the loss with every breath and every beat of my heart. I'd never again hold her in my arms. I'd never again hear her soft moans as I made love to her because even at its roughest, Sam and I had always felt the love from each other's touch. I couldn't bring myself to burn her body, but I couldn't conceive of burying it either. No option for her was good enough, or really, I just couldn't come to terms with actually letting her go—with taking that final step.

"We'll take her with us."

Nixon's eyes widened. "What? Where do you think we're taking her?"

"With us to kill Natalie, and everyone else linked to Project Reaper. When I'm done with all of them ... I want you to kill me." I ground my teeth together to keep another sob from escaping my chest. "I don't want to live without her. I can't."

Nixon pushed himself off the wall, his gaze boring into mine. "Then what? You want to be laid to rest with her like in some stupid Romeo and Juliet scenario? You've got to be fucking kidding me."

"I don't expect you to fucking understand."

"I understand being without her. I understand—"

"But you never really had her. You don't know what it's like to—" My throat closed up and the rest refused to be spoken. "Fuck," I finally managed. "I know you've been jonesing to kill me, just do it."

Nixon scowled at me. "And how are we going to transport her? We can't just stick her in the truck. She'll ... she'll—"

"I know about body decomposition. We'll pack her in ice. It'll preserve things long enough until we get back to West Virginia."

"You really want to do this?"

"Yeah."

I'd take out Project Reaper and everyone associated with them. And then when Sam was avenged, I'd find a way back into her arms. It didn't matter that it wasn't in this life, just as long as I was with her in the end. I should have known we'd never get a normal life together. In death was the only place we'd find peace, just like it'd always been for us.

Chapter 49
NIXON

"There," Austin mumbled as he pushed Sam's hair off of her face. His fingers slid slowly down her cheek, and then as if he'd been electrocuted, he yanked his hand away. I watched mutely as he closed the lid on the body-sized cooler packed with ice … and Sam. It was spread across the back seat of the SUV. The level of fucked-up-ness was off the charts. I tried not to think of the body as her, it was just an empty shell. Her soul had moved on. Still …

I shook my head hard. *No, I can't think about it.*

I walked around to the passenger side door and slid in as Austin moved to the driver's seat. He adjusted the rearview mirror down so he could keep an eye on the containment unit, or coffin really.

I was heartbroken, but Austin, I was pretty sure he'd lost all sense of sanity. For the first time ever, I began to wonder if I'd been wrong. I thought I'd loved Sam just as much as him, I thought I'd be willing to do anything for her, but I simply wasn't as broken as Austin. Or maybe we just dealt with grief differently. I found myself, much to my surprise, feeling sorry for him. He was beyond pathetic. He was barely functioning. I had a feeling if avenging Sam wasn't on his to-do list, he would already be dead, probably by his own hand.

"You shouldn't have killed him when you did. He had information. Information that we're probably going to need and don't have for getting into the compound."

What I hadn't told Austin was that I'd been able to siphon off just a bit of Malcolm's power before his death. I didn't have a chance to experiment yet, but I was pretty sure I'd managed to snag the art of illusion from him. How Malcolm obtained it to begin with was beyond me. Perhaps he could steal powers, too? Maybe it was genetic, which was a possibility I hadn't considered before. It was hard to believe someone like him had been my brother. It made me hate Natalie that much more. She'd created him. Hell, she'd created all of us. Mother or not, she deserved everything that Austin and I were bringing her way.

Austin hadn't responded to my comment about keeping Malcolm alive longer. I wasn't even sure he heard it. His eyes were glazed over, and he seemed to be turned internal, as if lost in his anguish. Me … I was getting angrier by the minute. The more I thought about everything, the more pissed off I got. There needed to be another word for how I was feeling. Things weren't supposed to go this way. Austin was the one that should be dead, and Sam and I were supposed to be together. I was going to give her whatever she wanted, I was going to save her—keep her safe.

"Fuck!" I swore as I punched the dashboard. I wanted to bring Malcolm back to life just so I could kill him all over again. He was ashes now though, dust in the fucking wind.

"Fifteen," Austin mumbled to himself. "It has to mean something."

I knew what he was doing. He was searching for answers where there weren't any. He was focusing on things to keep himself from losing it completely. "Tell me about this fifteen thing."

Austin's gaze darted to mine briefly, and he pressed his foot down harder on the gas pedal. "Sam kept having these dreams about people being killed in all these various ways—shootings or bombs, shit like that. She would see it from the perspective of one of the victims, but just before she died in the dream, someone would say fifteen. She felt like it was important. And she said it just before he ... before he—" He cleared his throat and swallowed, the sound thick. "It's important. I can feel it."

"Okay," I muttered.

The truth was, maybe she was having some kind of weird premonition. It wasn't one of her gifts, but Austin sometimes had visions. Maybe the power was diluted in her, and the vision had twisted to the point where she didn't understand it until her death. More than likely she'd been having visions about her own death.

"I'll figure it out," Austin grated, his knuckles whitening on the steering wheel.

I remained silent because I didn't think he was talking to me. I curled up against the window and crossed my arms. "Wake me up when you want me to drive." Closing my eyes, I prayed for a temporary escape from reality.

I STOOD AT A BUS STOP. *The small glass enclosure with the bench was stuffed with people, so I hovered awkwardly just outside. It was a ridiculously hot day, and the afternoon sun beat down on my overheated skin. Sweat dribbled down my spine, and gathered around my hairline, my clothes sticking to my body in random places.*

I glanced to my right, squinting, and noticed another enclosure identical to the one I was next to, a little way down the road. It was empty, offering a bit of shade and a chance to rest my legs. Without another thought, I walked over to it and sat down, heaving a sigh of relief.

No sooner had I settled in, than a loud screeching sound filled the air. Lifting my gaze, I spotted a UPS truck, out of control, and barreling down the steep hill overlooking the bus stop where I'd just been. The truck careened down the deep slope and lifted when it lurched over the crest towards the bottom. It was suddenly airborne and headed straight for the people who didn't have time to get out of the way.

The impact caused an explosion, one that rained glass and debris down on me. Lurching to my feet, I fled in a panic.

Screams thickened the air, and as I ran, people clamored around me, the same thing on their minds—to put as much distance between the bus stop and themselves as possible.

People were on fire, bleeding. I was the only one who was relatively unscathed. Without slowing my pace, I flicked my gaze over to a man who had smoldering pieces of burnt flesh hanging from his bones. He was something straight out of a horror movie. I shuddered with revulsion. Suddenly, he was much too close to me—

"Fifteen," his hoarse voice said, inside and outside of my head at the same time.

My world tilted, spinning out of control, and I opened my mouth to scream.

The next thing I knew, I was standing next to Sam, or rather a Sam-like image wavered over the body of a different person. She moved out of the body like a spirit, but her attention stayed focused on the corpse. I watched right along with her, getting the feeling that something important was about to happen.

After a few moments, Sam lifted her head to observe a black van approach. The body on the ground was scooped up, placed on a stretcher, and removed quickly from the scene. The van sped off, and Sam turned to look at me, her image wavering before shifting to that of someone else. The new person was a young girl, no older than her early teens, maybe thirteen or fourteen.

Her big, brown eyes gazed up at me with sorrow. "I tried to tell her. But visions were not her gift. I didn't see you until now."

"Who are you? What were you trying to tell her?"

"You have to find me. I can still save her. Just like I saved all of them. I'm at the compound. She'll be number fifteen. I want her to be number fifteen."

I jerked up from my reclining position in the SUV, my heart thrumming erratically in my chest. *Is it true? Is there a way to save Sam? Is there someone with a gift who can actually bring her back to me?*

I swung my gaze over to Austin. His eyes were glazed over as he stared at the road, speeding along. *Yes, to me.* I could help him exact revenge, kill him, and then have Sam all to myself. It would be perfect. Austin didn't love her more than me, he just loved her differently. She needed me. Austin was weak. He'd broken down, and I would be the one to fix everything.

I turned my head towards the window to hide the small smile that turned up the corners of my mouth.

Yes, things just might work out the way I want after all.

Chapter 50

AUSTIN

Nixon had gotten sloppy with his void shields, leaving himself completely vulnerable to me. Which was a good thing for all involved, or maybe that was a lie, but it was definitely a good thing for me.

I plucked the information from Nixon's head about the strange girl and what she communicated to him. Finally, what she was trying to show Sam in her dreams clicked into place. Natalie was harboring a person whose ability could bring the dead back to life. Of course that would be a closely guarded secret. It explained so much, including how Malcolm had been alive after I'd killed him. Apparently, Natalie had a soft spot for both her children.

I huffed out a shallow snort. *Nixon thinks he's going to take Sam from me after all?* I couldn't even muster up any anger at the moment about his ridiculous plans. Not when hope buoyed my soul at the prospect of getting Sam back.

It's not over yet. Thank fuck we didn't cremate her body. A knot twisted my gut, and I forced myself not to think about what could have been.

I'm going to get her back. A smile threatened to break across my face. I sucked my lips into my teeth to contain it. *Not having Sam is only temporary.* We would dismantle, body by body, Project Reaper, and then I would kill Nixon. Him and his entire bloodline had made our lives a living hell. Natalie, David, Malcolm, and Nixon … The world would be a better place when they were dead. And after they were gone, Sam and I could be happy. We'd find a way to make everything work, we'd find a way around our addictions.

I pushed the gas pedal down as far as it would go. I couldn't get to West Virginia and the compound fast enough. The sooner we got there … the sooner everything would finally be resolved.

Chapter 51

NIXON

Something in Austin abruptly changed. He was still quiet and focused, but he seemed … lighter somehow. I just hoped he wasn't planning something big that would blow back in my face and keep me from carrying out my plan. *What if he somehow inadvertently prevents me from finding the girl who could bring Sam back?*

Indecisiveness weighed heavily upon me. *Maybe I should tell him about the girl?* I could always get Sam away from him later. The most important thing was making sure Sam was alive and well again.

Shit, what do I do? Do I tell him or not? I waffled back and forth, pausing to try and force a vision to give me direction. Nothing was coming though. There was just a big, blank space where my future should be. When we finally crossed over into West Virginia, I still hadn't come to a decision. *Shit, shit, shit. What do I do?*

"We need to talk strategy," Austin stated calmly, breaking past my panicked thoughts.

Narrowing my eyes at him, I studied his expression for a clue of what he was up to. Because he was always up to something. His shields were too tight, and I couldn't get the slightest read on him. "What were you thinking?"

"Natalie sent you to kill me, right?"

"Yeah."

"So bring me to her."

I pursed my lips. "How do you propose I do that? Are you going to play dead? And she wanted me to kill you, not bring her back your body as a souvenir."

They'd shoot him on the spot. Which wasn't that big of a deal in itself, but I needed him for a distraction so I could find the girl that could bring Sam back to life. Austin couldn't die until I was ready for him to. "And she's going to think something's up that I'm back at all. I was going to kill you and disappear with Sam. The fact that I have you, Sam is nowhere to be found, and I'm not long gone … she's going to know something's up. We can't lie to her, remember? She'll have a ton of questions I won't be able to not answer."

"I remember what your dear ole' mommy's ability is. I'm open to suggestions if you have a better idea," Austin grated.

Shit. The thing was, I had the perfect way to get us into the compound. The problem was I'd have to reveal my ability to steal other people's powers. If I did that, then

Austin would have a better chance of figuring out my end game. But if I didn't tell him, Sam might stay dead, which was not an option. I really didn't have an actual choice; I was merely trying to convince myself I did. "Yeah, I actually do have a better idea." I heaved a huge sigh. "I stole a bit of Malcolm's ability. The one that he used to make himself look like you and me."

The SUV swerved a bit as Austin's head snapped to the right, his eyes narrowing on me with shock and anger. "What do you mean *stole*?"

"I can steal other people's abilities. There, I've said it. And the bottom line is—I can now make us look like whoever we want to get back in the compound."

"Did I ever actually know who you were? Or was everything a lie?" He ground his teeth together. "Were we even friends before Sam came along?"

Before I could think better of it, I let the truth spill from my mouth. "Sam was always there between us, even before you remembered her. Nothing good was ever going to come from us loving the same woman."

Austin's grip on the steering wheel tightened. "She never loved you back. You could have moved on."

"No!" I pinched the bridge of my nose. "I mean, no, I couldn't have. She's all I think about, all I want. I can't be happy without her."

"Yeah, well I guess you're going to die alone and unhappy," Austin growled.

The air between us filled with tension. Sighing heavily,

I stared out the window. "We can't talk about this kind of stuff now. We have a temporary truce—" And then his words sunk in. I pivoted in my seat to face him again. "Fuck me. You know, don't you? You know about …" *No. Stop. Wait. If he doesn't know then I could give it away if I say too much.*

Austin sneered. "Don't overthink what you're about to say. I already know what fifteen means and how that girl showed up in your dream to tell you."

My head dropped back, hitting the seat with a dull thud, and I clenched my fists in frustration. "How? How did you find out?"

"Someone forgot to double-check their void shields," Austin taunted. "I guess all the cards are about to be on the table, huh? I was planning on killing you, and you were planning on killing me, after Sam was alive again of course. Am I right?"

"Spot on," I growled. We were two peas in a fucked-up love triangle pod.

"All right. Let's face it, the only thing we can agree on is getting Sam's life back. I'll stick to the truce if you do. We both know that one of us is going to die by the other's hand when this is all over."

I nodded. "Fine. No more shady shit behind your back. When I kill you, I won't stab you in the back. I'll look you right in the eye when I do it."

"Sam might have something to say about that. You forget she doesn't love you."

"Enough," I spat, vibrating with anger. "No more talking until we get there or this is going to fall apart before it begins."

Austin clamped his mouth shut and ground his teeth together. I took that as agreement.

Chapter 52
AUSTIN

What else has Nixon been keeping a secret?

None of what Nixon did should have been a surprise because honestly, I would have done the same if I were in his shoes. I simply had to stay at the top of my game at all times to make sure I was the one who walked away with Sam when all was said and done.

Now that Nixon's secret power had been revealed, I knew exactly what his plan would be. He wanted to kill me, and then he'd use my memory-altering ability to keep Sam happily oblivious and with him for the rest of their natural lives. Was it necessary for the person to die to get their powers? I was guessing yes, otherwise he would have taken mine a long time ago. It would make sense that one couldn't steal someone's mental ability from them since it was a part of their genetic makeup. Taking it would kill them, but if they were already dying it could be stolen unnoticed. Of course, there were a lot of grey areas when it came to all of our talents, things that couldn't quite be explained, or shouldn't be possible, but just were. I'm sure there were scientific explanations for every last case, but I didn't know what they were.

"We're getting close," I said to Nixon who was staring out the window with a scowl on his face. "Who are we going to be?"

"I'll be me and you can be Malcolm."

"What?"

"Now that I know that we're both her sons … we'll go in under the guise that I just found out. Also, I can be all pissed off and well …" He shrugged. "It's the best I got."

It wasn't that bad of an idea when I considered it. If Nixon marched in with 'Malcolm,' hemming and hawing about finding out he was still alive, and his brother to boot, it would be the perfect cover. "It'll actually probably work." I glanced in the rearview mirror and my heart fisted. "What about Sam?"

"We'll carry the case in. I think I can hide it or make it look like something else. Cal did all kinds of crazy shit."

"I remember." I tried not to think about how Cal had tried to seduce me while wearing Sam's visage. The whole thing skeeved me out. I shook my head to dislodge the very disturbing memory.

Nixon sat up, motioning between us. "I should probably drive. Pull over, and we can switch."

I rolled the car to a smooth stop at the side of the road and got out to walk around to the passenger side. Nixon slid into the driver's seat, speeding off down the road the moment he was situated.

Nixon glanced at me several times before speaking. "I'm going to try and throw up the illusion now. I've never actually done it before, but these kinds of things are usually instinctual. Plus we're close enough to the compound that I'd rather be on the safe side."

"Makes sense," I said. "Let me know when you do it."

Nixon glanced furtively back and forth between me and the road, his brow furrowing in concentration. "It's done."

Yanking down the visor, I peered into the mirror. When I was met with Malcolm's reflection, I had to stifle the very real urge to smash the glass. I'd been friends with Malcolm once, too. Another family trait? I slammed the visor back up and tried not to picture Malcolm inside of Sam. It didn't matter, none of it would matter now that he was dead and I'd be getting my wife back.

"Good job," I uttered harshly.

Nixon grunted. "Let me do most of the preliminary talking."

"I can handle being Malcolm."

Nixon snorted. "I'm sure you can."

I decided not to take the bait. I knew exactly what he was trying to imply, and it was a crock of shit. There was a difference between being confident and arrogant. Malcolm and I were nothing alike. I stared straight ahead as the gates to the compound loomed up in front of us.

Adrenaline pulsed through my system and my palms began to sweat.

"Here we go," Nixon muttered under his breath.

I gripped the door handle and sent up a silent prayer. It was time for us to end things, one way or another.

Chapter 53

NIXON

I had no idea what would be done to me if we were caught. Would Natalie's patience finally run out when it came to my antics? Really, I had nothing to lose except my life, and that was for shit anyways, especially without Sam.

"Hey," I said coolly when I rolled down the window at the front gate.

The guard strolled up to the side of the SUV brandishing a military assault rifle. I internally chuckled. As if that could stop us. He'd never know what hit him if we didn't want him to. This was a finesse operation though. Otherwise, we could ruin our only chance to save Sam.

Recognition washed over the guard's face. I might not know him, but he certainly knew who I was. "No one informed me to be on the lookout for you."

Ignoring the guard's comment, I pushed forward. "Inform Natalie that both of her sons are here to see her."

The guard's eyes widened slightly as he noticed 'Malcolm'. I wasn't sure if he knew him by reputation or by sight, or possibly both. "Go ahead. I'll phone ahead to let her know."

"You do that," Austin rumbled.

As we moved from the SUV and unloaded the case that Sam was in, I paid special attention to every minute detail to make sure no one saw what we were doing. We walked right in the front door as if we should be there. In fact, we marched in looking mightily pissed off, which was to be expected under the circumstances.

Natalie met us just inside the entrance of the compound. Austin and I settled the case on the ground next to the wall, which was relatively out of the way.

"I didn't expect to see you back here, or with him in tow." She motioned towards Malcolm.

"I didn't expect to be back here at all." And I hadn't expected to be, which made me able to say it with her truth-forcing ability. I thought I'd be halfway to Bora Bora or some other paradise-esque location with Sam by now. The trick to out-smarting Natalie's ability was to always tell the truth. It was all about being careful of how much you said and the words you chose. I'd had years to perfect my technique.

"So you know?" She eyed me warily.

I narrowed my eyes at her. "Yeah, and I have questions."

She clicked her tongue. "Where's Austin?"

"Alive."

She tilted her head quizzically, as if my answer confused her slightly. "All right. I guess this conversion is long overdue. Both of you come with me."

Austin glanced at the case, which only we could see, and I nodded once to let him know that I was pretty sure I could keep it concealed since we weren't going far.

We followed Natalie to her office, and she hastily ushered us in. It was all very civil if not predictably awkward.

"Now, what is it that you wish to know?" Natalie asked as she situated herself behind her desk, and we settled into the chairs on the other side.

I'd start with the obvious question I both wanted to know and she'd expect me to ask. "Why didn't you tell me about Malcolm?"

She drummed her nails along the top of her desk. "I knew you'd be upset. But what I want to know is how you found him and how you found out that he was your brother at all. Truth is, I hadn't expected to see either of you again."

Interesting. "You didn't think you'd see Malcolm again?"

"No, he'd become too much of a liability." She glanced in Austin's direction. "We had his memory wiped."

"Obviously that didn't work," Austin growled.

Natalie's eyes darkened with disgust as she addressed Austin who she thought was Malcolm. "There was nothing more we could do for you, Malcolm dear. You were beyond redemption and too far gone to be of any use. It was only my soft spot for you that saved your life at all."

"I thought you and David wanted different things. I thought—" I started, but Natalie didn't let me finish.

"I've always wanted different things from David. He was all about the money, and the government contracts. I wanted to keep our country safe. I wanted to help people."

"Help?" I recoiled in shock and disgust. "Help who exactly?"

"Yes, help. Between my separate operation where—"

Austin burst up from his chair, his chest heaving. "You fucked all of our lives up. You treated us like lab rats. Who is that helping?"

"It's for the good of the country, for the good of the whole. A few suffer for the safety of many."

"What's your grand plan now, Mother?" I spat, hoping to derail Austin before he said something to give us away. "All your hopes and dreams were pinned on Austin as the perfect assassin for your little project. What happens now that—"

"We're cleaning house. With the exception of you and your brother, we're moving on to new subjects and new methods. Austin and Sam … all of the children from that batch, are failed experiments. They're a danger to society and need to be eliminated. I'm sure you can understand."

"What about me getting Sam once I killed Austin, was that all a lie?"

Natalie's face softened slightly. "No. It's my fault you're

so obsessed with her. I know you can keep her under control. With Austin out of the way, there won't be a repeat performance of him coming for her."

A chill ran up my spine. "What do you mean it's your fault?"

Austin was now sitting perfectly still as well.

"It was another experiment gone wrong. Most of the empath pairs bonded naturally on their own, and under the circumstances became very co-dependent on each other. Our concern was what would happen if one of a bonded pair died. We experimented with trying to force a secondary bond if that were to happen."

My hands curled into fists, my body trembling as I fought to stay in my chair. "You made me obsessed with Sam when you knew she had some kind of special connection with someone else?"

"I'm sorry. You already liked her, I just thought—"

Rage burned me from the inside out. "You're sorry?" I choked out, spots dancing in front of my eyes. "You're fucking sorry?"

Austin rose from his seat, shooting me a look. He started for the door, and I made sure it appeared like he, or Malcolm, was still sitting in the seat next to me. I would deal with Natalie while he made sure Sam was brought back to life.

"Nixon, please. You're going to get her. You're going to—"

"She's dead." The words just spilled from my mouth. *Shit.*

Natalie gasped in genuine surprise. "How?"

"Your other son, whose memory was very much not erased, was hell-bent on making Austin feel exactly what he did when Maggie was stolen from him."

Her piercing gaze shot to Malcolm. "And you didn't kill him?"

The corner of my lips tipped up. "Oh, Malcolm is very much dead. And he's not coming back this time. I made sure to burn his body." I let the mirage of Malcolm fade away slowly, dramatically.

"What have you done?" she exclaimed.

I rose from my seat, stalking slowly towards her. "I'll tell you what I've done. I've come to resurrect Sam, and I've brought your death with me."

She sputtered as she tried to figure out what to do and say to convince me to change my mind. "Nixon, please, I'm your mother."

I laughed. "You may have given birth to me, but you were never my mother. All the things you did … I'm not even sure you're human."

"I did it all for the good of the country. For the good of—"

"And I'm going to kill you for the good of mankind." I raised the pistol I'd had at my back, aiming it straight at her head. "I'll see you in hell … Mother."

I squeezed the trigger.

Chapter 54

AUSTIN

Adrenaline propelled my body to move faster than I wanted, despite my worry of drawing unwanted attention to myself. Skidding to a stop at the makeshift coffin Sam was in, I paused only a moment to check for any unwanted visitors before awkwardly dragging it down the hallway.

I wasn't sure where I was going precisely, but I was fairly confident the girl we were looking for was locked up in one of the cells on the level where Sam was held the last time she was here. Reaching out my senses, I didn't have to wait long before connecting with exactly the person I was searching for.

"Find me," a young female voice lilted directly into my head. *"Bring me my fifteen."*

An image danced across my mind of a girl sitting cross-legged in a nondescript hospital room. The familiarity of it hit me. *Is this compound where we were all held as children?* I thought we'd been in Pittsburgh. Apparently, I was wrong. Memories from my childhood of torment cascaded through my brain, releasing the knowledge of where I needed to go.

Nixon darted down the hallway from behind me, catching up quickly. "Come on, we need to hurry. She's dead. Natalie's dead." Showing zero remorse about his mother's death, he picked up the pace, panting heavily. "I'm stretching myself thin. I'm not sure how much longer I can keep all these illusions going, so we need to get Sam taken care of before anyone finds Natalie's body."

We hefted the coffin up between us, and Nixon followed my lead without asking if I knew where I was going. He trusted me when it came to all things Sam. He knew I would never risk losing her permanently.

"Here. Keep coming. The last door."

I followed the directive from the girl, pushing into the last door on the right at the end of the hospital wing. Before we even could catch our breath, the girl from Nixon's vision approached us with a wide smile on her face. Despite her youth and welcoming demeanor, her eyes held a deep despair I was sure was put there from being in this place and under Natalie's 'care'.

The girl was already opening the lid on Sam's makeshift coffin before Nixon and I settled it fully on the ground. She reached inside to rest her hand on Sam's forehead. A low humming sound, more of a buzz, registered in the recesses of my brain as the girl threw her head back, face scrunched in concentration.

Is something happening? How long is it going to take? I stood frozen, my gaze glued to Sam for any sign of revival. *Fuck. What if Sam was dead too long? What if she can't be saved after all? What am I—*

Sam erupted from the sloshy ice she was packed in, choking and sputtering as she sucked oxygen into her lungs.

She's alive. Sammy, my Sammy girl, my beautiful wife is alive. I found myself beside her, reaching out to run my fingertips gently around her neck. *No more protruding bone from the break. She's alive and healed. I wanted to believe—but a part of me—it's a fucking miracle.* I wrapped my arms around her, yanking her out of the ice.

"Austin? I had the weirdest dream. I dreamt that—" She clutched at my shoulders, her hands fisting my shirt. "No … I was dead. I was dead, wasn't I?" She pulled away from me to face the girl, her savior—mine as well. "It was you." She nodded slowly, a silent communication passing between her and the girl. "I understand now."

"You will set us all free," the girl said, her smile widening. "I knew I wanted you for my fifteen. I'm just sorry I had to let Cal die. He had to in order for everything else to work. I told the dark side of Alex and he understood." Her smile wilted around the edges.

Shit. Now I understand, too. The girl had something to do with why I'd killed Cal and how the number fifteen had been associated with it. That information normally would have caused unparalleled rage within me—that I'd been controlled yet again. But not at the moment … at the moment I couldn't take my eyes off her—my Sammy girl.

The thing I wanted most in the world was to sweep her up into my arms to disappear forever with her, but I knew it wasn't that simple. Nothing was ever that simple with us. We had to clean up the loose ends of our past so they couldn't trail along behind us anymore.

"Sam," Nixon croaked from behind us.

Shit. I forgot he was there.

Sam glanced in my direction before stepping past me to stand directly in front of Nixon. "I know it's not your fault. I know you can't let me go because of what Natalie did to you. But you have to know, Austin is who I love. Nothing will ever change that."

It took Herculean strength not to pull her back into me. I needed to feel her very much alive body against mine. I needed to taste her, to touch her—I just needed to feel her life emotions. Those, at least from her, were more addicting than any death emotions.

"Sam," Nixon choked out her name again. He turned his head as if he couldn't look at her anymore. "I'm sorry. I'm sorry for everything." He raised a handgun to point in my direction. "It's for your own good."

Sam's face hardened. "No."

Nixon slammed into the wall behind him, the gun clattering to the floor. Sam whirled around, meeting my gaze with hers. "It's finally time to finish this." The hairs on the back of my neck stood on end as I watched her glide smoothly from the room almost as if she was floating.

Nixon remained where he'd been thrown, his gaze tracking her until she was out of sight.

The girl covered her mouth with her hand and giggled. "She's going to free us all."

Chapter 55

SAM

I *was dead.* The concept was difficult to accept, and I was sure when I stopped to think about that fact, I would have some kind of emotional breakdown. Now wasn't the time though. No, now was the time for me to put an end to Project Reaper once and for all.

I finally understood that every choice and every path had been leading me to this moment. I was here because I could do what no one else could. I would become death, the perfect assassin, the Grim Reaper they'd all been hoping for but with consequences none of them saw coming.

A piece of me was now switched on that had been off before my death. I felt whole and complete, *and I knew* Chloe and Samantha were no more, they had merged. I was simply me. And because of it, I had a new kind of control over my abilities that I never had before. How ironic that the very thing Project Reaper had wanted was going to be the thing that destroyed them. Ultimately, they created the method for their own demises.

My senses crept out from me like tentacles, reaching and twisting, searching for everyone in the building. I could feel all of them, all of their emotions, and all of their thoughts. I would kill all that were responsible for the torture of innocents. I knew that technically I was about to murder hundreds of people in cold blood, but I couldn't bring myself to care. I didn't even consider them as human. Not one of them had been unaware of the horrors that were taking place right under their noses. None of them deserved life. Not when they tortured the innocent.

I moved down the corridor, seeing what was in front of me, but focused on the minds I was rifling through.

I'd been wrong, there was one guard—he'd been appalled, and he tried to help when he could. He didn't leave because he couldn't; he knew they'd make him disappear. He wasn't like the rest. I'd spare him and only him.

"Go," I whispered in his mind. "Run. Get out of here." I pushed an image at him of everyone dead or dying around him. His horror curled through me, and he abruptly made the decision to obey. He sprinted towards the front of the building, completely panicked. One of the other guards tried to stop him, demanding to know where he was going. He pushed past his co-worker to make it out and he kept on running.

I smiled to myself. *Now it's time to get down to business.*

In my mind's eye, I imagined that I was connected to

everyone with dark, shadowlike fingers radiating from my core. I was able to feel and see what everyone I was attached to was thinking and feeling, and I also could push things down the line into them. Like the dark, insidious ball of energy I was gathering inside of me. It would kill them all, and I didn't even have to be in the same room as any of them.

"Sam," Austin murmured from behind me. He poked gently at my mind with his. It was his way of asking for admittance.

I let him in as he wrapped his arms around me, pressing his hard front to my back. Leaning into him, I allowed my eyes to slide shut. Austin hissed in a breath when he realized what I was about to do. His anticipation for so many deaths hummed within both of us.

I released the tangle of dark energy, savage delight swirling through me as I pictured it traveling down the psychic links to explode in each person at the other end. Screams of agony and fear erupted within me in a macabre melody that serenaded me and Austin both. I groaned in pleasure, gripping Austin's hands in mine. This would be the ultimate high. Nothing could ever compare. We both knew it. No one, not one single person, had expected what was being done to them, and most had no clue that it would result in their death.

"Help me!"

"Please, stop … What's happening?"

"One of those freaks has to be doing this, oh God!"

So many deaths. So much to feel. Bliss. Pure bliss.

"Austin," I whispered, turning within his arms. With my eyes squeezed tightly shut, I lifted my face to him, searching for his lips. He snagged them with his, and I moaned, reveling in his taste. The lust from him crashed into me in waves, beating at my already ultra-sensitive skin. I no longer held any coherent thoughts … I was all emotions … all I could do was feel. And I felt everything.

Austin's tongue danced with mine within the wet heat of my mouth. His callused hands skimmed down my body to fondle and knead. I pressed myself into him, his muscles taut with tension. I was almost overwhelmed with how much I needed to feel him inside of me.

Plucking the thoughts from my mind, Austin lifted me up and slammed me into the wall behind us. Even the pain served to heighten my desire. People were dying around us, I was killing them, and I wanted to feel just how alive I could be. *I was dead … I was dead. And now I'm alive. More alive than I've ever been before.*

A strangled cry burst from me, tears streaming down my face. Austin's anguish from experiencing my death was still razor-sharp. There was a part of him that almost couldn't believe I was back.

He tore my pants from my body, the sound of the material shredding echoing in my ears, and he plunged into me in one harsh stroke. I threw my head back, digging my nails into his shoulders. As he began to move inside of me with punishing force, the death emotions that surrounded us caused my mind to splinter off into memories of our life together, poignant moments.

I felt drawn to explore what was in the room I was in front of. I slid inside silently, making my way to the bed by the window. A beautiful boy lay there, the moonlight from the night spilling across his face. His nearly black hair was sticking up in all directions, and he blinked open the bluest eyes I'd ever seen.

"Who are you?" he asked.

I was hit with a feeling of knowing, almost like someone had reached down into me and placed information into my head. "You're going to be very important to me. And I'm going to be just as important to you."

I slapped my hand over my mouth with horror. Why would I say that? It was embarrassing to say such things to a stranger.

He frowned at me. "I know."

I peered at him thoughtfully. "What do you know?"

He shrugged. "Not sure. It's like the words just slipped out of my mouth."

His sadness washed over me, yanking me down into the murky depths of his emotions. I was used to knowing what other people felt, but I'd never experienced it so clearly before. I didn't merely feel his sadness—I was now sad, too. "Why are you so sad?"

His eyes widened with surprise. "A-Are you like me?"

I began to fidget nervously. I'd slipped up again, and yet there was something about the hope in the beautiful boy's eyes when he asked if I was like him. Maybe I was, and then maybe I'd actually found someone I could share my secrets with. "Like you how ... sick?" I hedged.

He smiled at me, showcasing a dimple that made my heart

speed up. This beautiful boy was definitely my new crush. 'What's his name' from my kindergarten class was old news.

"No, can you feel stuff about other people?"

"Yeah," I breathed.

"And you just sometimes know stuff like about the future?" His face and emotions had morphed into hope. Maybe he had secrets he wanted to share with me, too.

"Well, I don't really know stuff about the future." I shuffled back and forth beside his bed.

"Oh," he said. "But you said we'd be important to each other. That was about the future."

I grinned. "Yeah, I guess it was."

"I'm Alex." He hopped down from the bed, standing only a smidge taller than me, but Mom told me boys were slower developers than girls. I hoped Alex would grow up to be tall so he could be my boyfriend.

"I'm Chloe."

"So, what are we doing?"

"Oh, well, my roommate, Kevin, and me were going to spy on stuff." I shrugged. "His idea, not mine."

Alex's smile brightened. "I like it, let's go."

He reached out his hand for mine, and I slid it into his. The minute our skin touched, the two of us gasped in unison. My head swam with his thoughts, and I could tell his was doing the same with mine.

We spiraled into darkness together.

It was the first time I ever laid eyes on Austin. Even then I sensed what he would come to mean to me. We bonded naturally, and through torture our connection had been tempered to become an unbreakable force. Even when my mind had been wiped clean, and I didn't hold any of the memories of us meeting as children … my love for Austin hid him in the recesses of my soul. Our minds had temporarily forgotten but our hearts never would.

Austin's nostrils flared, the only warning that his control had snapped. He shoved me against the wall, his hand gripping my throat tightly, as his lips seared mine. I grunted in dismay even as I met his desperate tongue with matched fervor.

His hand flexed against my throat as he ground against me, my leg already hooked around his waist. His touch burned and soothed, excited, and calmed my inner turmoil because maybe our being together was a betrayal and a mistake, but it was my betrayal and my mistake, all of what I was doing my choice with no outside emotions cluttering my mind. And I wanted this —him like I never wanted anyone or anything before.

"I need you, Chloe." Austin's heated breath skated over my flesh as he kissed his way down my neck.

"Yes," I moaned, throwing my head back to allow him better access. "I need you, too."

"We need to go somewhere." He'd somehow managed to get my shirt up, capturing my nipple between his teeth. "Can't do this here."

"Your room," I rasped.

"No … Jessica," he said around my other nipple.

Irrational anger caused my gut to clench. Then I remembered Nixon. He was waiting for me in my room. Guilt replaced every other emotion.

I pushed at Austin's chest. "No, Austin, we can't. What about Nixon? He's your best friend."

Austin's voice was low and gruff with unspoken promises of pleasure. "I need you."

He offered me no other explanation, no argument, no rationalizations, just that he needed to be with me, plain and simple. And I wanted it—oh how I wanted it. I wanted him in any and every way he would let me have him.

We'd hurt so many people along our journey. I'd done things I wasn't proud of, but I couldn't bring myself to feel ashamed. Everything was grounded in my love for Austin. I couldn't fathom that being a bad thing. Even tainted, our love for each other was still pure, and I would always do whatever in my power to preserve it.

It's beginning.

The lives I was taking had entered the crescendo of death, their emotions spilling through us with a heightened intensity.

In response, Austin pistoned against me, his flesh slapping into mine harder and faster than I thought possible. I clawed at his shoulders, my inner muscles spasming around him.

Then the final notes of the death emotions ripped through us …

We screamed in pain, in pleasure, in ecstasy and torment. We were torn apart and put back together all in an instant.

It abruptly dropped away, leaving us alone in each other's minds. The faint buzz of the prisoners bustling with excitement lingered, knowing they would soon be free.

But it was all so far away. It was just Austin and me, our minds dancing languidly together as we stared into each other's eyes, panting heavily.

No words needed to be said, but they fell from my mouth anyways. "I love you, Austin."

His lips twisted up in a familiar cocky smirk, showcasing his dimple. "Yeah, I know."

Chapter 56
NIXON

Sam glided from the room with death on her mind and she wasn't even attempting to hide it. She'd woken up different … *darker*. But I couldn't be bothered to care; she was alive again and that was all that truly mattered.

She'd sliced into me deep though, twisting the knife when she'd looked me directly in the eyes and told me that she loved Austin. She'd uttered those same words probably about a million times before, but this time, for the first time, I'd really heard it—felt it.

I should have left, regrouped … something, anything other than standing frozen in the room with the girl that had brought Sam back to life. I heard and felt them all dying around us, the people responsible and connected with Project Reaper. Sam was doing that, and Austin was with her. I knew what that would ultimately lead to. My entire body stiffened with the knowledge.

A small, clammy hand slipped into mine, startling me. I stared down to see the young girl peering up at me curiously. "She will set us free, but you will give us our lives back."

What's that supposed to mean? Fuck if I care right now. Clearing my throat, I said, "What's your name?"

She stood straighter, seeming to puff herself up. "I'm Hallie."

I crouched down so I was at eye level with her. "What do you mean I'll give you your lives back?"

"They've altered us, changed us. Just like with Sam. We'll never be able to have normal lives unless you help us. We deserve to live."

Just as I was about to ask who these other people were, a handful of young children crowded into the room, dashing hand in hand to surround Hallie. Excited chirps and laughter filled the air.

"My God, you're all children."

I knew that Sam hadn't been more than six or seven when she'd been taken, and I'd still consider that a child, but one of the kids, a boy, looked to be no older than four. The people of Project Reaper truly were monsters.

Hallie smiled at me with confidence. Like she'd known me her whole life or I was some kind of superhero. "You can take their abilities and then no one will want to use them anymore."

I shook my head, understanding what she wanted. "The process will kill them."

Her grin grew. "And I'll bring them back."

I blinked rapidly. "You'll bring them back," I repeatedly numbly, my mind reeling at the prospect.

"Yes. You make them normal. Make it so they can live happy lives, and I'll give them that life."

"What about you?"

Hallie's smile wavered around the edges. "Nothing can be done for me."

It was surreal to be talking to someone so young about such things. Hallie's eyes held so much sorrow and pain, and yet she smiled like it didn't touch her. Her body might be young, but her soul was ancient.

"What will happen to me? That's a lot of power for one person." But it would give me more options, too. With that amount of skill, I could take Sam, like I always wanted, if I didn't go mad first.

Hallie ignored my question and dropped my hand. "We'll start with Benjamin." She walked over and picked up the smallest boy, the one who looked like he was only about three or four. His dark brown curly hair stuck out in disarray, and his bright blue eyes studied me intently. Hallie set him down in front of me. "Go ahead."

Benjamin reached his hand out for me, and I took it. "You sure you can bring him back?"

"Positive," Hallie said with utter confidence.

I reached in with my ability and ripped Benjamin's power away. I'd never tried to steal an ability from someone who wasn't close to death before. It was more difficult, as if the power held onto Benjamin, resisting with each tug. When it finally flowed into me, Benjamin's small mouth opened in a silent O, and he crumpled to the ground. I sucked in a breath at the sight of the small boy dead on the floor.

"Do it, Hallie. Bring him back." I couldn't look away from the crumpled form in front of me.

Hallie bent down, stroking her fingers over Benjamin's face, and the air changed, as if electricity was humming through it. Benjamin's eyes flew open a moment later. Sitting up, he grinned from ear to ear, his gaze moving from Hallie to me.

"How do you feel?" Hallie asked him.

"I-I'm … I can't hear any of your thoughts anymore." His grin grew impossibly big, taking over his entire face.

Warmth bloomed in my chest, and I rubbed my hand over it. Benjamin now had the potential for the type of life I would forever strive for. He could grow up, fall in love, and maybe even have children of his own. The possibilities were endless, and I had given him that. I'd given him a chance at a normal life.

My mind once again turned to Sam. She was death and I was life. Two sides of the same coin. I swallowed back the bile in my throat. What if I could give her what she truly craved? What if I could give her and Austin a normal life? Could I really be that unselfish after everything I'd done to keep her?

I was yanked back to the task at hand as Hallie presented another child to me, this one a girl about the age of ten or eleven. Her long, blonde hair reminded me of Sam's strawberry blonde curls she'd had when she'd been about that age. My heart quadrupled in time. Suddenly, an image of Sam was superimposed over the girl, and as I ripped her ability from her and watched her smile in glee once she was resurrected … I knew what I had to do.

Chapter 57
SAM

The death emotions had come and gone, the afterglow lingering. Austin and I were lying in the middle of the hallway, wrapped around each other, our legs and arms intertwined. Our connection had never been as strong, as if we truly were one heart and one soul, lost in each other both physically and mentally.

And I was happy, content. Except …

Except for the small, niggling feeling that was already stirring in the dark recesses of my mind. *What happens now with my death addiction?*

For the moment I was satiated, but I knew there would come a time when I wanted more—when *we* wanted more. I might have single-handedly put an end to Project Reaper, but now I was more of a danger than I'd ever been before. What would we do when the dark cravings took over and there was no one to keep me in check, no one to stop me? No one to stop us?

"We'll figure it out." Austin's firm lips moved against the sensitive skin of my neck.

"We should check on the girl and the others that were held here to make sure they're okay."

Austin nodded against me, and we rose slowly to our feet.

My knees wobbled as an image of Nixon slammed into me. *Oh my God—* "He's killing them!" I blurted in shock, taking off at full speed with Austin close at my heels.

Skidding to a stop, I clutched at the door frame, my eyes wide. *I can't actually be seeing this.* Nixon was crouched over a little blonde-haired girl who was dead on the ground. *He killed her. Why did he kill her?*

It doesn't matter. Rage swept me up and propelled me forward. I surrounded Nixon within the tight grip of my power, and he doubled over in agony.

"Sam, no … you don't understand," he rasped. "Hallie said … I'm helping—" His words were cut off as he curled into a tight ball on the floor trying to escape what I was doing to him.

"No!" several tiny voices cried out in unison.

My gaze was pulled over to the girl who had brought me back to life. I hesitated, and Nixon groaned as my hold on him loosened.

"I don't understand. He killed … he—"

The girl who'd saved me stepped forward, swiping her hands over the dead girl, and a moment later her eyes flew open. She met my gaze, her eyes liquid. "We want this—to be normal."

"Hallie asked m-me to. I'm h-helping," Nixon sputtered. "I take their abilities, and Hallie brings them back."

I blinked rapidly, understanding dawning. My hands dropped to my sides, and Austin stepped forward to pull me into him.

"They want to have everything we couldn't," he whispered in my ear, the scruff on his face abrading my cheek.

I shivered.

Tears pooled in my eyes. Nixon shoved off the ground, managing to force himself into a crouch. The girl, whose name I now knew was Hallie, ushered a different child in front of Nixon, this one a boy. I watched in grim fascination as Nixon tore his abilities away, and Hallie brought life back into his tiny body. With each child, a relieved kind of happiness shone from their eyes upon resurrection that hadn't been there before their death.

When all the children had their abilities stripped, all except Hallie, Nixon turned to meet my gaze. His dark chocolate eyes slid over me with pain and want, anger and remorse. I was what he could never have. Even if he stole me away from Austin again, I would never truly love him the way he wanted … the way he needed.

"I'm sorry," he rasped. "I never meant to cause you— I love you, Sam. Even though I went about it all wrong from day one."

I glanced back at Austin, and then stepped away from him and into Nixon. I cupped the side of his cheek, his skin warm against my palm. His eyes slid shut for a moment as he nuzzled me gently. "I never meant to hurt you either. The heart simply wants what the heart wants. I guess that applies to both of us."

Unbidden, the memory of what had started it all, or at least had felt that way at the time, slammed into me.

"Don't do that," Nixon growled.

Smiling innocently, I batted my eyelashes. "Do what? You said you wanted me to dance for you, so I am."

"You know what I mean," he snapped. "Don't do it like you don't know me."

"You mean, don't dance for you like I'm Raven? Do I sense a little resentment? Did someone forget that I'm supposed to be undercover? You should consider yourself lucky that you're getting a dance at all with me being on a case."

Focusing on Skyler, I attempted to open myself up to her emotions again, but it was pointless with Nixon being so close. His void abilities were completely blocking my empath gifts. Instead, I went with plan B, otherwise known as the dumbest choice possible.

Austin. I conjured an image of him in my mind's eye. Wrapping myself in his essence, I shivered with delight. Nixon no longer lounged on the couch in front of me. Instead, Austin's azure gaze glittered with lust as it met mine. Yes. You, I want to dance for.

The music pulsed through me, my heart rate dancing steadily along with the beat as I undulated my body and swiveled my hips. Mmm ... yes. My temperature seemed to spike, the power I was holding over Austin heady. I slid up his body, pressing tightly against him, inhaling his spicy scent. So good. I wanted to lick every inch of him, map the ridges and planes of his body with my tongue. I wanted—needed to taste Austin.

Straddling him, I leaned over to whisper in his ear, "You like that, baby?" I ground my hot center against the hard erection pushing against his pants, letting out a moan.

His hands slid up to cup my ass, grinding me into him with force.

Grabbing his wrists, I flung his hands away. "Huh-uh. I told you the rules. I can touch you, but you can't touch me." I placed his hands on the back of the couch, rewarding him with a swivel of my hips.

Austin's eyes sparked with a dark lust. "Sam ..."

I stilled, shooting him a glare. "That's not my name anymore. If you want me to play, then I'm Raven to you here and nothing else."

Indecision rolled through his eyes before lust finally won out. "Yeah. Okay. Raven."

"That's better." I punctuated my words with a slow grind against his crotch. I let the music pull me under again, carrying me away to a place dominated by my desires. Sliding back down to my knees, I ran my hands up his inner thighs to cup him. I wanted to hear Austin's moans of pleasure as I took him into my mouth. I wanted to taste his vulnerability while he touched the back of my throat. And most of all, I wanted to swallow him down when he finally came, all while he couldn't

touch me. I wanted—needed complete control over him, and I would have it.

The sound of me undoing his zipper caused him to jolt upright. "What are you—"

I slid his entire length into my mouth in one go, stealing his words as I choked on him. He fisted my hair, but I reached up and flung him away from me. This is my show, baby.

I licked and sucked him while using my hands to stroke and cup. I swirled my tongue, loving the taste of him, lost in the act of giving him pleasure. Too soon, he spilled into my mouth, and I moaned as I lapped up every last drop of what he gave me. After it was over, I was reluctant to let him go, but I did.

Shakily making it to my feet, I gazed down at Austin who was slumped back on the couch. His hands gripped the cushion above his head, and his pants were undone, his cock glistening from my saliva, red lipstick ringing the base. I loved seeing him like that, knowing I'd been the one to unravel him so completely. His heavy-lidded gaze followed me as I reached for my beer. Taking a sip, I let some of it dribble down my chin before wiping it off with the back of my hand. I set the bottle down so I could pull up my gown. "I'm leaving now."

My words set him into motion. He stood abruptly, struggling to get his pants zipped. "Wait, Sa— Raven. I bought you off stage."

"I'd say that was well worth what you paid for." I strode out of the room with him hot at my heels.

"Raven, I said to wait," he grated, reaching for my arm.

"You don't get to tell me what to do." I glared at his offending

hand, shaking it free. "And you never touch me without my permission."

"We need to talk." His eyes flashed dangerously.

"No. I'm done talking, or didn't you notice? I gave you what you wanted. That should make you happy. But you don't get to fuck this assignment up any more than it already is."

"What do you want from me? Tell me, Sa— Raven."

I stared up into Austin's baby blues, blinking in confusion as they faded to a deep chocolate brown. No longer was my fantasy lover standing in front of me. Not Austin. Nixon.

A wave of dizziness washed over me, and I staggered on my ridiculously high shoes. "I'm not doing this right now, Nixon." I had to say his name to remind myself who he was. "I'm on a case, and you shouldn't be here. Go home, don't try to follow me."

I'd wanted Austin over Nixon even when I was convinced that Austin was a figment of my imagination, and Nixon had made me believe he was my real husband. Nixon always wanted me … and I always wanted Austin. And our fucked-up love triangle wasn't even fully our fault. Natalie had a hand in it. She'd had a hand in all of it. She'd ruined both of her son's lives, and nearly mine and Austin's as well. The world was going to be a better place without her in it.

I swallowed around the lump in my throat. "Austin and I are going to disappear. Please, Nixon, if you really love me you won't try to stop us, you won't—"

Nixon broke away from me, a hysterical laugh bubbling up from his chest. "If I really love you? *If?*"

Austin moved in close behind me, his body heat radiating into my back. "We should go," he murmured, tension riding his tone.

"No!" Nixon exclaimed. "You need to make sure the children find their way back to their parents. You have to promise me you'll do that."

I noticed Hallie was staring at Nixon with a sad smile plastered across her face. "I knew you'd understand," she whispered, tears glistening in her eyes. "I knew if she was my fifteen that you'd understand."

I tried to push into Nixon's mind to decipher the interaction between them, but his shields held tight. "Nixon …" But my words lodged in my throat when he reached out to touch Hallie.

"Thank you," she whispered.

The other children had all begun to cry, and the thick, desperate level of emotions in the room was threatening to strangle me. Austin pulled me up into his arms, speeding towards the exit. I saw Hallie crumple to the ground from the viewpoint of over his shoulder. *But wait. If Nixon stole Hallie's power, then can't he just bring her back? Why all the dramatics?*

"No," Nixon whispered in my mind. *"Her gift is not meant to exist in this world. It's too much power for one person."*

"Stop!" I shouted at Austin. "Just stop!"

Hesitantly he obeyed, dropping me down to my feet. I grabbed his hand, turning back to face Nixon.

He'd flashed it into my mind, showing me in an instant what he planned to do. It wasn't about Hallie at all. She would be brought back. It was about him. He was going to save me after all. Austin and me both. *He really does love me. But I can't let him. It wouldn't be right.* "Nixon …"

"Shhh …" he croaked. "Just take care of the children. And be happy, Sam. Be happy."

He raised his gaze to meet Austin's, who was standing perfectly still, his chest rising and falling unevenly. "We were friends once, I think. It would be nice if you remembered me that way."

Austin nodded, his Adam's apple dancing up and down in his throat silently.

"Okay, let's do this." Nixon smiled with false cheer.

Nixon's fingertips skimmed my temple, and in the millisecond before everything went black, Nixon shared with me everything he ever wanted to tell me but never could.

He loved me—more than anyone or anything. I never should have doubted it. If only someone could have loved him back just as much. He deserved so much more from this life. He would forever be my biggest regret because I would wish for all of eternity that I could have saved him just like he was about to save me.

I JERKED AWAKE, fully aware. I felt … I felt only me. I lifted my gaze to Nixon, who was standing in front of me, a sad smile tipping his lips up, and unshed tears shimmering in his eyes. "I did it all for you." He lifted the handgun to his temple and squeezed the trigger.

A scream tore from my chest, and I crawled across the floor to his body. The bullet had gone through one temple and out the other, a drop of blood dribbling down his handsome face. I stared into his empty eyes—eyes that had loved me more than I'd been able to comprehend until the very end. He'd given up everything for me, and all I'd ever done was hurt him.

I choked on my sobs, guilt and regret overwhelming me.

There were still so many unanswered questions, like how did Nixon form a permanent bond with me, but I hadn't formed a lasting one with him? At least not the kind I had with Austin. How had there been so many people and things in play that we hadn't been able to pick up on, even with our abilities? In the end, I guess it didn't really matter. Besides that, they were all dead, and dead men tell no tales.

Austin pulled me away from Nixon's body and into his arms. He stroked his hand through my hair and down my back. "It'll be okay, Sam. He made his choice. He was our friend. He was." Austin's voice was thick with his own sorrow, but he held back the tears for my sake. I couldn't feel it, I felt nothing but my own emotions, but I knew.

Austin and I owed everything to Nixon.

"We need to take care of the children. We need to make sure they find their way home."

I nodded against his chest. "And then we can start our

life together." Nixon had made his choice. He'd died so I could live. I intended to do just that. I'd live every day to my fullest and never forget what he sacrificed for me … for *us*.

"Yeah, we can finally start our normal life together." A laugh sprung up from him. It sounded young and carefree, even though we were standing in a building surrounded by death. "Us normal? I'm not even sure if I know what that means anymore."

"It means that it's just me and you. And it means that you can't poke around in my mind without my permission anymore."

Doubt swelled up within me. What if Austin and I had come to rely on our abilities too much? What if we couldn't make it without them? What if we succumbed to problems that regular couples did, like lack of communication? After everything, what if we destroyed ourselves with normalcy?

"I don't have to be an empath to feel your worry. Death itself couldn't come between us. A little bit of normal isn't going to tear us apart—*my* beautiful Sammy girl." Austin pressed his lips against mine in a chaste kiss, probably not wanting to scandalize the children.

I smiled against his mouth, reassured by his words and actions. Despite everything that happened, Austin and I were finally free, and we hadn't lost everything in the process. We still had each other. That would never change. His love would always be felt with every breath I took.

Acknowledgments

As an overthinker, acknowledgments are quite an arduous task for me. I wonder if I'm being lackluster or too intense with the thanks. Or did I forget someone? Possibly I gave too much credit to someone and therefore slighted someone else who actually did a ton. A part of me doesn't want to include these in my books at all because the people I appreciate should know it already … or do they??? No matter how I look at it these damn acknowledgments make me friggin' sweat.

But here they are anyways since if I don't include them then people will probably think I'm ungrateful and weird. I mean, I am weird, but I don't want people to think that. I am grateful though, so I'll just go-ahead and make this uncomfortable for everyone. Heh.

Okay, here I go. Right now. Actual acknowledgments to follow. Hopefully, they represent an appropriate level of gratitude to all the people in my life that deserve it.

(And yep … I have totally copy & pasted what comes next from my *Replayed* book acknowledgments, which I originally took from *Virtual Reality Bites* acknowledgments. I thought maybe after *Replayed* that I'd come up with something better. Or at least something new. Obviously not. So this is now copy & paste edition #7. Or 8? 9? Who even knows anymore. Therefore, I'm thinking you should probably get used to it.)

My amazing Hubby! Words can't begin to explain how supportive and truly amazing he is. Hmmm … I think I already used the word amazing. But unlike in books, when honestly applied to someone, the word amazing means something, well, amazing. And my hubby is all of the things that word implies. Romance heroes are nothing compared to him.

Lindsay Tiry … what would I do without you? I hope I never have to find out. From cover design to interior graphics to logos, you do it all. Your talent is awe-inspiring, and I hope one day everyone else will be able to appreciate how you shine.

Melissa Ringsted … my illustrious editor. Without you, this book probably would have gone straight into the trash. Thank you for giving me the confidence to publish when I convinced myself that I was the worst writer in the history of writers, and for fixing all the words.

Ren, Kristin, Shona, Ruty … my O.G. chicas … I wouldn't be here without you. I'm beyond lucky to know all of you.

And last, but certainly not least, thank you to everyone who has taken the time to read this book. Hopefully, you enjoyed it, but even if you didn't, I still appreciate the fact that with so many options out there today, you even gave my book a fleeting chance.

About the Author

Ava Wixx escaped into books at a young age and decided to stay there. It was only a matter of time before she was driven to create her own fantasy worlds from fear of running out of places to explore.

Reader, writer, dreamer ... Ava only toils in reality when absolutely necessary. She lives in North Carolina with her husband, and spoiled mini-poodle.

www.ingramcontent.com/pod-product-compliance
Lightning Source LLC
LaVergne TN
LVHW041103080826
845145LV00007B/1671

* 9 7 8 1 9 5 5 9 5 0 3 3 6 *